*A Tugging String*

*Also by David T. Greenberg:*

DON'T FORGET YOUR ETIQUETTE:
THE ESSENTIAL GUIDE TO MISBEHAVIOR

THE BOOK OF BOYS (FOR GIRLS)
AND THE BOOK OF GIRLS (FOR BOYS)

YOUR DOG MIGHT BE A WEREWOLF,
YOUR TOES COULD ALL EXPLODE

THE GREAT SCHOOL LUNCH REBELLION

WHATEVER HAPPENED TO HUMPTY DUMPTY?

CROCS!

SNAKES!

SKUNKS!

BUGS!

SLUGS!

# A Tugging String

**A NOVEL ABOUT**
**GROWING UP DURING THE CIVIL RIGHTS ERA**

## David T. Greenberg

DUTTON CHILDREN'S BOOKS

**DUTTON CHILDREN'S BOOKS** | *A division of Penguin Young Readers Group*

PUBLISHED BY THE PENGUIN GROUP

Penguin Group (USA) Inc., 375 Hudson Street, New York, New York 10014, U.S.A. | Penguin Group (Canada), 90 Eglinton Avenue East, Suite 700, Toronto, Ontario, Canada M4P 2Y3 (a division of Pearson Penguin Canada Inc.) | Penguin Books Ltd, 80 Strand, London WC2R 0RL, England | Penguin Ireland, 25 St Stephen's Green, Dublin 2, Ireland (a division of Penguin Books Ltd) | Penguin Group (Australia), 250 Camberwell Road, Camberwell, Victoria 3124, Australia (a division of Pearson Australia Group Pty Ltd) | Penguin Books India Pvt Ltd, 11 Community Centre, Panchsheel Park, New Delhi - 110 017, India | Penguin Group (NZ), 67 Apollo Drive, Rosedale, North Shore 0632, New Zealand (a division of Pearson New Zealand Ltd.) | Penguin Books (South Africa) (Pty) Ltd, 24 Sturdee Avenue, Rosebank, Johannesburg 2196, South Africa | Penguin Books Ltd, Registered Offices: 80 Strand, London WC2R 0RL, England

This book is a work of fiction. Names, characters, places, and incidents are either the product of the author's imagination or are used fictitiously, and any resemblance to actual persons, living or dead, business establishments, events, or locales is entirely coincidental.

Copyright © 2008 by David T. Greenberg

The publisher does not have any control over and does not assume any responsibility for author or third-party websites or their content.

CIP Data is available.

Published in the United States by Dutton Children's Books,
a division of Penguin Young Readers Group
345 Hudson Street, New York, New York 10014
www.penguin.com/youngreaders

*Designed by Heather Wood*

Printed in USA | First Edition
1  3  5  7  9  10  8  6  4  2
ISBN 978-0-525-47967-3

41028837    4/09

To my father who has stood by me
through thick and much thin:
the man I most admire
    Love,
    Duvy

# A Tugging String

# Preface

Every other year in elementary school we took a field trip to the Hayden Planetarium at the Museum of Natural History in New York City. There, a whirring machine that looked like an enormous robot ant, capable of walking into the audience and gobbling children, projected star maps on the domed ceiling. An announcer, using a flashlight with an arrow-shaped beam, outlined constellations. It amazed me that only a few stars in the same region of sky would form the basis of Pegasus the Horse or Ursus the Bear or Orion the Great Hunter. The constellations were dots in the sky around which early man wove wonderful, imaginative patterns and stories.

The following story of my childhood and my father's role in the civil rights movement is just such a constellation. It is not a scholar's rendition of history; it is fictional. But it encompasses many fixed stars of historic and personal fact. I have drawn a constellation around actual events and personalities from the 1960s civil rights movement and my own experiences, hoping to illuminate them and bring them to life.

# I

*1960*

The Orange Blossom gave off a familiar, comforting smell of diesel and rain. Jack Greenberg frowned at a shaving cut in the stainless-steel mirror above the stainless-steel sink. He reached for the doorknob, missed, tried again, and stumbled out of his roomette eight cars back from the engine. This was a bad section of railroad track, and the Orange Blossom resented it. Greenberg knocked on the door of his boss, Thurgood Marshall, and the two of them walked like sailors on a pitching deck, down the lurching corridor to the dining car. Out the window a lightning flash illuminated the train's silver tail curving along the trestle spanning a tumbling Georgia river.

"What river is that?" Greenberg asked a passing Pullman porter.

"Why, suh, that's the R-R-R-R-R-appahanock."

Aware that Pullman porters tended to label all rivers as the R-R-R-R-R-appahanock, Marshall stifled a grin.

—◦◦◦—

People stared when the two men, one white and one black, entered the dining car. A lady in a round, red silk hat as fancy as a Valentine candy box spilled her drink on the linen tablecloth. One family abruptly got up and left. Some diners showed no interest.

"A nigger," whispered a man with a neck wattle.

Ten years before, the Supreme Court had ruled it discriminatory and illegal to prevent blacks from eating in train dining cars, yet still there were whites, especially in the Deep South, who were upset by this.

"What may I get you, Mr. Marshall?" asked one of the waiters.

Marshall and Greenberg ordered, indifferent to the hostility around them. "Jack, when I leave the NAACP Legal Defense Fund to become a judge[1], I need to propose to the board of directors a director-counsel to succeed me."

---

1. John F. Kennedy appointed Thurgood Marshall to the United States Court of Appeals in 1961. In 1965, Lyndon Johnson appointed him solicitor general, to represent the United States in the Supreme Court. In 1967, Johnson appointed Marshall to be the first black Supreme Court justice.

Greenberg nodded. Salads, wedges of iceberg lettuce, were placed before them.

"There are a number of excellent lawyers I have considered. But after much reflection, I have chosen you."

Greenberg rested his glass, its water sloshing slightly to the judder of the train.

"There will be objections that you're white and that I have a responsibility to pick someone who is black and that I was pressured to select you. But the simple fact is that our organization is devoted to racial justice. I believe you are the best person for the job. You're not only a superb lawyer, but you are also extremely capable of handling complex, emotionally charged situations. And your color should be no factor in my choice. I'm confident the board will confirm my decision."

Greenberg looked down and noticed that his salad, on a blue plate with a chipped rim, had a large dead fly on top of it. As the waiter passed, he asked for a new salad. The waiter picked up the plate and Marshall put his hand over it, stopping him. "First bring him another salad, then take this one," he said. For Marshall, a former dining-car waiter, knew that the man would take the salad into the kitchen, remove the fly, and just bring it out again. Greenberg sipped his water, slowly nodding his head. A new salad was brought; the chipped plate removed.

"I will do everything in my power," Jack Greenberg said, "to earn the trust with which you honor me. Thank you, sir."

"Greenbug," said Marshall, gently punching his arm with affection, "if you ever need help, call on me."

The waiter passed them with a wide smile on his face, bearing a salad plate—blue with a chipped rim—for the man with the wattle.

"And how is your family?" asked Marshall.

"Thriving," Jack Greenberg said. "Thriving."

# II

## Fall 1964

"Why is everyone here Negro?" I asked, keeping my face forward and expressionless, but shifting my eyes back and forth rapidly. My father, whose office door said DIRECTOR-COUNSEL, NAACP LEGAL DEFENSE FUND[1], was driving me diagonally across Great Neck, a route I'd never before taken, to my touch-football game. I was wearing shorts, and the skin on the back of my legs was stuck to the green vinyl seats. Every

---

1. In the sixties, Southern states sued civil rights organizations. State legislative investigations harassed them. Southern states tried to disbar civil rights lawyers in Virginia, Mississippi, and Florida. At a minimum, this interference was disruptive. At a maximum, such organizations could have been put out of business. The NAACP Legal Defense Fund was headquartered in New York City, out of reach.

time I moved my bare legs, they sounded like the plastic wrapper unpeeling from fruit leather.

We had left our section of town, with brick and stucco homes separated by trimmed hedges, and now drove alongside concrete apartment buildings that looked like tall, decaying bunkers left over from a war. I was startled by how completely different this place was from my neighborhood, and yet how close. Enormous patches of paint, like old cabbage leaves, peeled from the buildings. The buildings were separated by scraggly lawns, with clotheslines zigzagging everywhere like rubber bumpers in a crazy pinball game. Some of the clotheslines, though I couldn't figure how, had been stretched from one building's upper-story window to the next, farther than you could easily throw, and clothes dangled like ships' flags all the way across. Ragamuffins madly raced plastic trikes. Older men sat still on benches staring out at the street, some leaning against canes. And young men, tense and jittery, stood by themselves or in small knots.

Now and then, passing cars would stop near them and the men would lean in the open windows. Even though I was with my father, I was scared. I locked my door and rolled up my window, but slowly so it might not appear obvious. I knew black people, but none like this. We had a housekeeper, Sally, who came once a week. She wore a white uniform, had a ring on every finger, and, I was astonished to discover, on each pinkie toe. During breaks she would sit on a dining-room chair and silently move her lips as she read from a stapled book titled *Psalms and Miracles*. She cleaned, cooked, and yelled at me in a Jamaican accent, "Wachoo doin', mon?," for making messes, just like any other adult. I knew my dad's old boss, Thurgood Marshall, and lawyer colleagues of my father who were black. But they were just grown-ups, too. I saw black people in New York City, working as bus drivers or janitors, but they were so distant from my life I didn't think about them at all. Nor did I ever stop to think about the two black students in my school one year ahead of me. The people outside my car window were different, newly discovered next-door neighbors without clothes dryers, edgy, alien, and I felt curious and frightened at the same time.

"Lock your door, Dad," I whispered, staring straight ahead. "Dad!" Casually he did. "Where are we?"

"These are the projects, Duvy," my father said, mild as always. "The poorest section of Great Neck, and these are the poorest people in Great Neck. Most cities and towns in the North have an equivalent to this."

"Equivalent" was dad language. He taught part-time at Columbia Law School in New York City and often spoke with dictionary words, a style I tried to copy.

"But why are the poorest people all black? You'd think there'd be some whites mixed in with them."

"Will you listen if I give you a long answer?" my dad asked.

"Yes," I answered. "And don't pick your proboscis; Mom hates that." We hit a bump and my legs unstuck for a minute, making the same *slurrrp* as a wet shower mat being pulled up from the tub floor.

"The Negroes here are poor. And they're poor because

they don't have jobs or they have the lowest-paying jobs. They don't have the skills needed for good jobs because they are uneducated."

"But why?" I asked. "All they have to do is go to school and they can do anything they want." I'd heard these words from my parents so many times that they were like an in-home Pledge of Allegiance.

"You go to school and I went to school," my father said. "But the history of most Negroes in America has nothing to do with school. Most of the Negroes arrived here in the North only in the last twenty years. Before that they mainly lived down south. And before that most lived in Africa. They were brought as slaves from Africa to the South."

"But that was so long ago," I said.

"Slavery ended only about one hundred years ago," my dad replied. "That may seem like a long time ago to someone who just turned twelve, but it's less than a flicker on the human time line."

We pulled up to a red light. There was a young man on the curb muttering to himself. He wore a Harvard sweatshirt that was far too tight, and an Afro pick in his bulbous hair. "Uh, Dad," I said. "Dad, um, he's walking toward us."

"Don't worry," my father said, annoyingly cool. "When he sees you, he'll turn around." And he was right. The man took several more steps, caught sight of me, and abruptly reversed to his perch.

"Who is he?" I asked.

"Drug dealer," he said. "You're obviously not a customer. As

I was saying, Negroes were brought here as slaves. They were treated like work animals. Their owners purposefully prevented them from getting an education, even punishing them if they read or tried to read, in order to prevent them from gaining opportunities and acquiring wealth—in other words, from gaining equality."

"But weren't the Negroes freed near the end of the Civil War?" I asked.

"Yes," my dad said. "But then came the Ku Klux Klan and Jim Crow to enforce the values from before the war." He blinked his eyes twice, his habit when unhappy or disturbed.

The projects behind us, we pulled up to Grace Avenue Park, thronged with children in colorful team outfits. I was a blue Tiger. I unpeeled myself from the front seat, leaving a reverse pattern of genuine fake, nonslip leather upholstery on the backs of my legs. My father said, "Don't forget, Mrs. Sutherd is driving you home. Say hello to her for me."

**III**

I dismissed the projects from my mind and concentrated on the game. Catfast, great reserves of strength untapped, I barely broke a sweat and knew, *knew* I would score. From a distance I heard yelling, whistles, howls. I dodged and dodged again, furiously accelerated . . . touchdown! I turned to my teammates, who just stared at me. I wasn't known for making touchdowns. In fact, I'd never made one before in my life. I was exultant.

My teammate Leo Jones yelled, "You idiot, you fool, you doofus! You ran the wrong way and you just made a touchdown for the other team!"

"Yeah, Greenberg, they won because of you!" shouted Paul Ferber.

Kids all around me were hooting, pointing. Coach chuckled. I heard the word *jerk*. Tears overspilled my eyes. I wiped them with my sleeve and they spilled again.

I was not thriving. The problem was that I wasn't good at anything. Not anything important. I was pathetic at all sports. I couldn't play an instrument, sing in tune, draw, do magic tricks, or tell jokes. I had repulsive curly hair that, despite my purchase of the "Miracle Comb" ("Your hair won't roam with the Miracle Comb"), no amount of combing would "train" straight. I read science fiction and magazines about gizmos and gadgets, which made me a nerd. My reflection in a mirror suggested I was physically visible, and yet to other kids I just wasn't there. At best I was "Greenberg." It's not that I wanted to be popular, though I hoped that kids might like me. I wished to be noticed, to be someone.

Mrs. Sutherd, who lived up the street, and who gooped on her makeup, dropped me at home. "Is your dad in town for a while?" she asked.

"I'm not sure. I hope so," I said. "And he says hello to you."

"Do you know what your dad does?" she asked.

"He's a lawyer."

"Do you know what kind of lawyer?"

"Civil rights lawyer."

"Do you know what he does, though?"

"He helps Negroes, I guess." I was eager to go in and I could tell this was meant to be another of her instructive talks, which were, like her makeup, applied poorly. Her last one was about the importance of lighting Shabbat candles every Friday at sundown, something she knew we didn't do, and I was in no mood.

"But do you know the exact kind of work he's doing?"

"Nope."

Mrs. Sutherd looked at me, wrinkled her nose, and smiled. "You should read the *New York Times*."

"I do."

"Not just the sports section. Well, tell him hello back and that our rabbi and congregation believe in what he's doing and to stay safe. And hello to your mom."

"Okay, Mrs. Sutherd."

I joined my dad on the porch. "How was football?" he asked.

"Great," I said. "I scored a touchdown. Hi from Mrs. S. Her rabbi likes you even though you don't light candles and she said to stay safe, ha ha."

My dad looked up a moment. "Hmm," he said.

He absently ruffled my hair. His legal papers were spread out all around him, *The Collected Poems of Edward Fitzgerald* perched atop a law journal. I picked up *Popular Science*, my favorite mag. *Popular Science* was filled with articles about such things as wristwatch televisions, family submarines, nuclear-powered homes, or colonizing Venus. I was intensely interested in colonizing Venus and often pondered the question of how to deal with the Venusians that Dr. Schleger of Midwest Technical Institute speculated existed. (Based on his analysis of the planet's chemistry, they must look like octopuses, but be green, land-based, and hostile.) I began re-reading an article about the technology of the coming decade, "Cars That Turn into Airplanes."

Mom poked her head in. "Lunch."

"I'll make it myself," I said.

"No, I'll make it for you."

"No, I know just what I want."

"There's a poem in here I think you'll like," my father said to me, lifting the Edward Fitzgerald book.

Mom said, "Lunch first."

"Okay," I instructed. "I'd like two pieces of lightly toasted rye bread with caraway seeds." My mother started tapping her finger on the door frame. "On top of the first piece of bread put a thin layer of chunky peanut butter, then a layer of banana, and be sure to slice it the long way, and then a layer of honey from the small jar, NOT the large jar." My mother's tapping frequency increased and her eyes narrowed, but I heedlessly proceeded. "And then, please take a bag of potato chips, toss them in two tablespoons of garlic butter, and bake them for about ten minutes at three-fifty until the butter is absorbed." Garlic potato chips were my newest invention.

Clenching her jaw muscles and scrunching her eyes, my mom said, "You may make it yourself."

Ezra, my little brother, who was playing with blocks in the living room, called, "Peanut butter jelly."

"And what do you want for lunch?" she asked my older brother, Josiah, who'd just walked by. My brother's hair was very long, almost covering his ears. When our Hebrew school teacher disapproved, my brother said that it wasn't as long as Moses', which got him kicked out of class for disrespect.

"Do you have a salami sandwich?"

I had begun crafting my sandwich when I heard CBS Radio announce, "This is Dan Rather reporting from Saigon. In the aftermath of a battle that has raged all day in the highlands outside of Hue, there are eighteen American dead, one hundred and ninety-two Vietcong." "Vietcong" was the name for the Communist soldiers fighting us in Vietnam. *Great*, I thought, *we're winning*. I tossed my chips in garlic butter and preheated the oven.

Then, "Malcolm X, leader of the Black Muslim movement, a movement that openly advocates violence against whites, said today at a rally in Harlem" . . . I concentrated on my garlic chips, but heard an angry voice speaking from the radio. Words filtered through. Did he actually say *hate the white man, separate from the white man*? I paid closer attention. The voice became angrier, and I actually stepped back from the radio. It said that whites just wanted to use blacks, just wanted to make money off of blacks, wanted to exploit blacks. I was shocked and turned the radio off.

I was white. I wondered why Malcolm X hated me. I'd never met him. I had nothing against him. My mind skipped to the projects and I felt a prickly sensation, as though there was a connection. I was scared of Malcolm X. I was scared of the people in the projects. Did they hate me, too?

My mother screamed, "What do you mean you don't want a salami sandwich? You asked for one, I made you one!"

"I didn't *want* a salami sandwich!" Josiah yelled back just as loudly. "I just wanted to know if you *had* one." There was a loud thud and Josiah ran out, Mom in hot pursuit, the sandwich flying through the air as if ejected from a cockpit. Our boxer, Heidi, gleefully scampered after Mom, tail vibrating, nipping at her sneaker laces, nabbing salami.

I walked back onto the porch, where my father, unflappable in the midst of mayhem, was making edits on a typed paper. He put his papers down, motioned me to sit beside him, and put his arm around my shoulder.

He opened the book of poems and said, "It's called *The Rubáiyát of Omar Khayyám of Naishapur.*"

Savoring my sandwich and garlic chips, I listened as he read:

> *"Awake! for Morning in the Bowl of Night*
> *Has flung the stone that puts the stars to flight*
> *And Lo! The hunter of the East has caught*
> *The Sultan's Turret in a Noose of Light."*

There was considerable banging upstairs that distracted me, but my dad dramatically read on, and I heard:

> *"The moving finger writes; and, having writ,*
> *Moves on: nor all thy Piety nor Wit*

*Shall lure it back to cancel half a Line,*
*Nor all thy Tears wash out a Word of it."*

There was a *boom* from upstairs. His expression unchanged, Dad glanced upward then continued reading to the conclusion.

"The 'Bowl of Night,'" I said. "Why a bowl?"

"What shape is the sky?" my dad asked. "Is it flat? Does it curve? Which way does it curve?" He swung his hand above his head.

I shivered, for I could see the sky now as an infinite bowl, the stars and we ourselves points within it. Separate and connected, all within the arc of space.

"But what do you think 'the moving finger writes' means?"

My dad thought for a moment and said, "I think the poet is saying that life is written for us or our destiny is controlled by a higher power."

"Do you believe that?" I asked.

"No. I believe we have control over our destinies and we can make a great difference in our lives and the lives of others."

I considered this.

And my father went on to say, "Words, correctly used, are extraordinarily powerful, each one a lever. In this way, poets and lawyers are alike."

We were silent a moment. I cringed as I thought of my humiliation at football. I thought of airplane cars. An airplane car would certainly make life better for my father. He wouldn't have to take the train for his business trips anymore, and he could spend more time with us. We could fly to Grace Avenue Park . . . over the projects. The projects. I pondered our earlier discussion as we drove through the dilapidated neighborhood, on the way to touch football.

"What's the Ku Klux Klan?" I asked my father.

"The Ku Klux Klan," he said, and then he paused a moment to consider his words and to fumble with a defiant buckle on his briefcase, "is an organization started by Southerners who felt they were treated unjustly by victorious Northerners at the end of the Civil War. They felt Northerners illegitimately imposed their views and values upon them, including the belief that blacks should be treated equally with whites. Many of them believe that Adolf Hitler—leader of Nazi Germany during World War Two—is a hero for loudly declaring that the white race is superior to others, particularly Negroes and Jews. They dress in ghostly-white robes and terrorize Negroes who do not toe the line. They're still an active organization."

"And who's Jim Crow?"

"You mean *what's* Jim Crow. Jim Crow is the unofficial name for a set of laws that segregate blacks from whites. The name comes from a popular minstrel dance from the 1800s that mocked blacks. Blacks down south where I travel are not allowed to drink from the same water fountains as whites, not allowed to use the same restrooms, eat in the same restaurants, swim in the same pools. Some public places are segregated in the North, but it's virtually the rule in the South."

This was a discussion we'd never had before and I was shocked. "Why do they feel this way?"

"It is a holdover from before the Civil War and perhaps back to the dawn of time. Many whites, because their parents taught them, simply believe that blacks are inferior, do not deserve equal privileges, and must be kept separate. Early in my career, when I took the train anywhere in the South, and even up north, with Thurgood, he was not allowed in the dining car. It was only a few years before you were born that blacks and whites could eat together on a train."

I knew Thurgood, my father's former boss, the "mastermind," as my father said, of *Brown v. Board of Education*[1], in which the Supreme Court ruled that all segregated white schools in the country must desegregate; my father had helped argue the case. Thurgood came out to our house some weekends with his wife, Cissy, to watch basketball games. He shot hoops with my older brother in the backyard, and sometimes affectionately called me "knucklehead." I couldn't believe that he wouldn't be allowed to eat in a dining car with my dad. "No way," I said. "That was in the old days. Not now. I don't believe you."

"You'd better," my father said. And in his professor's voice he said, "The law changed because of a 1950 Supreme Court case called *Henderson versus United States*. The Supreme Court said that separate dining cars for blacks and whites violated the Interstate Commerce Act, which states that all those

---

1. In 1954, in *Brown v. Board of Education*, the Supreme Court held that school segregation was unconstitutional. In 1955, it said that desegregation should be enforced with "all deliberate speed."

who pay the same fare must be treated the same way."[2]

I considered what my father said. It seemed unthinkable that some people *nowadays* thought that other people, simply because of their color, were inferior. In the past, of course, but not now. Then I remembered about World War II and how six million Jews had been killed simply because they were Jews. So perhaps it was possible. But that was in Germany before I was born, not today in the United States.

"How long until you have to leave again?" I asked. There was more crashing and screaming from upstairs.

"Weeks, months maybe," he said, and hesitated. "Mom's just wound up a bit right now. Don't worry."

"Why is she wound up?" Mrs. Sutherd's words, *Tell him to stay safe,* came back to me.

He hesitated, started to speak, hesitated again. "Well, sometimes people feel stressed."

---

2. Thurgood Marshall and my father helped prepare a "friend of the court" brief for the case. The Supreme Court decision described railroad dining cars with ten tables exclusively for white passengers and one exclusively for Negro passengers. A curtain separated Negroes from the others. Only four Negro passengers could be served at one time and only at the table reserved for Negroes. Other Negroes had to await a vacancy at that table, even when there were vacancies elsewhere in the diner. Whites also had to wait whenever more than forty whites wanted service at the same time and the table reserved for Negroes was vacant. The Court decided that the rules violated the Interstate Commerce Act, which makes it unlawful for a railroad engaged in interstate commerce "to subject any particular person . . . to any undue or unreasonable prejudice or disadvantage in any respect whatsoever."

*Crash.*

"JACK, DO SOMETHING!"

He sat several moments, blinked, and then slowly headed up the stairs past Heidi, who pulled her lips back in a hideous grimace and growled . . . protecting her salami.

# IV

## Dorothy Milton Tries to Register to Vote

If you wanted to vote in Selma, Alabama, you had to register to vote in Selma, Alabama. And there was just one place to do this: the Selma Voter Registration Office. The office was on a run-down side street, a few blocks west of the main post office, with several vacant lots nearby. A line of crabgrass, invulnerable to all weed killers, grew in the crack between the office and the sidewalk. Whites entered through a glass door on the right with the word WHITES on it. Blacks entered through a glass door on the left that read COLOREDS. Behind each of the doors were roller blinds the color and texture of great-grandmother skin, cracked in places and stained darkly here and there, as though by age spots.

A year ago, the first time Dorothy Milton had come to register, the "Coloreds" door had been locked, even though several whites went in and out of the "Whites" door. Sensible as she was smart, aware of how dangerous it would be for her to use the "Whites" door, she knocked on the "Coloreds" door to get in. The white women working within did not look up or respond. She knocked and rattled the doorknob and still they ignored her. Dorothy, who wore a silver brooch in the shape of a rose, looked despondently at the fringe of grass between the sidewalk and the office. Between the green blades were tiny, almost microscopic flowers with jewel-like red and purple petals. She contemplated them, smiled to herself, and left.

A month later, when Dorothy returned to register, the clerks inside again ignored her. Before she left, Dorothy gave the door a sharp kick. One of the women inside looked up and stared at her blankly. Then she peered at the license plate of Dorothy's car and made a note on a piece of paper. Several days later Dorothy's husband, Hector, told her that Mr. Decker, his boss at Gallagher's Farm Machinery, had taken him aside for a talk. Decker had heard that Hector's wife was stirring up trouble, and he would have nothing to do with it. He liked Hector. But either Hector's wife would stop, or Hector would be fired.

"They can fire me if they like," Hector said to Dorothy. "They've done worse to others, far worse. I will not be threatened."

"Are you sure about this?" Dorothy asked.

"As sure as a blue boar's bushy bristles," Hector replied, kissing her. "There are bills to pay, though, and if I'm fired, it's going to be rough."

"I know, sweetie," said Dorothy, stroking Hector's cheek and looking intently into his eyes. "But Decker votes. His mousy secretary votes. Most white adults vote. I'm one of the few among them with a college degree, and I can't. Granddaddy was a slave, couldn't vote. Pop was a sharecropper, couldn't vote. It boils my blood. How dare they stop me!"

When Dorothy went to register again, this time wearing a dress with a lovely pattern of daisies and daffodils, the "Coloreds" door was unlocked. She entered and stepped into an office sour with boredom and cigarette smoke. And yet, like sun through majestic rain clouds, light pierced the cracks of the blinds in dusty shafts, giving the room a holy air. A small plastic radio softly played accordion music. Oscillating fans asthmatically exhaled one way and then the other. The "Colored" side of the office had cigarette butts on the floor, the "Whites" side none. Two other blacks, a man and a woman with lunch boxes in their laps, sat next to each other and kindly smiled at her.

Dorothy walked up to the counter and said politely, "I would like to register to vote."

The woman behind the "Coloreds" side of the counter, taxidermied by cigarette tar, coughed several times, grimaced, and said in a husky voice, "You'll have to sit in the waiting area until we're free to help you."

"How long do you think that will be?"

The woman didn't respond, but dragged on her Kent and tapped the ashes into an overflowing ashtray, formerly a spittoon.

"How long do you think that will be?" Dorothy asked again into the smoke.

The woman linked eyes for a moment with her partner behind the counter, on the "Whites" side, swiveled back to Dorothy, and sharply said, "Sit down, girl. I'll get to you as soon as I can. There are others ahead of you."

Dorothy pushed her fingers against the counter so her fingernails turned red and tightly smiled. "All right. Fine. I'll wait. You let me know when you're ready."

Straight-backed, Dorothy sat for two hours and fifteen minutes on the plastic seat in the section reserved for "Coloreds." As she sat there, several whites came in and briskly conducted business. Finally she got up and walked over to the clerk, past the other two blacks, who gaped at her. With elaborate politeness she said, "Excuse me, I've been sitting here for two hours and fifteen minutes. In that time, you haven't been busy with anything at all. May I please have the paperwork that will allow me to register to vote?"

The woman behind the counter sighed and examined her fingernails. "In order for you to register to vote," she finally said, "you have to complete a questionnaire to prove you're qualified." She handed Dorothy a folded paper stamped in black ink with the words *Colored Voter Registration Form.*

Dorothy went back to her seat, removed a pencil from her purse, and opened the form. Her major in college had been history. And, anticipating a challenging test, she had recently taken a night course at her church. She was quite familiar with U.S. history and Alabama history and the federal and state constitutions. There was only one question on the form, however. It had been typed, not printed, by a typewriter with a defective *b*. Dorothy read it and squeezed the armrest tightly. She blinked back tears, shook angrily, and looked up appalled at the lady behind the counter, who looked back without expression. Dorothy broke her pencil in two. Then she tore the form into confetti, held it up high, and dropped it in an ashtray, whirling the dust within the sunbeams. Several whites in the office looked at her with astonishment and indignation. Dorothy stalked out.

—◦◦◦—

"Can you believe the gall of it? Can you believe it!?" she said. She paced back and forth in her kitchen, stopping now and again to press her palm into the counter. The room was filled with potted flowers, Dorothy's passion. Hector watched her thoughtfully as he shucked peas into a yellow plastic basin.

"I am not, I is not, and I ain't giving up," she said.

Hector listened.

"*Brown versus Board of Education* is just a court case in Washington. It hasn't made much difference down here.[1] The schools are still segregated. And the Klan still does what it wants when it wants and no one stops them. The only way we can make things better down here is by electing leaders who

---

1. Only in 1969, when the Supreme Court decided *Alexander v. Holmes County Board of Education*, a case argued by my father, did the Court rule that school integration had to be immediate.

are fair and honest to Negroes. They don't want us to vote because they don't want us to elect fair people. For my sake, Granddad's, Pop's, and for the sake of our children, I cannot let that happen."

"Make no mistake, they've got you marked now," said Hector. "If you go back again and try to register, the consequences may be rough. Remember my cousin Chauncey? The Klan burned down his house and barn after he tried to register. And after Pastor Wilks's brother registered, a couple of Klan boys beat the stuffing out of him and his other brother, too. And remember little Ham Hamilton? Best student in our grade. When he tried to register they gave him that crazy literacy test. Told him no problem, he could register, but first he had to answer whether 'the state could coin money with the consent of Congress.' He got that wrong, so he tried again to register. This time they asked, 'Name the rights a person has after he has been indicted by a grand jury.'[2] Wrong answer again." Hector paused and rubbed his mustache. "You know I'll stand by you, though."

Dorothy looked lovingly at her husband and rubbed away

---

2. Both of these are actual "literacy test" questions administered to blacks. Others include: "Where do presidential electors cast ballots for president?"; "Name one area of authority over state militia reserved exclusively to the states"; "The power of granting patents, that is, of securing to inventors the exclusive right to their discoveries, is given to the Congress for the purpose of _____"; "The only legal tender which may be authorized by states for payment of debts is _____." Do you think you could answer these questions? Another infamous literacy test question was "How many seeds are there in a watermelon?"

tears. "You always have," she said. "Can you drive me next week?"

"Yes. And will you tell me now what the question was on the form? Maybe I know the answer. I may not have your college degree, but I am after all a man of culture and class, good-looking, and beloved by dogs."

Dorothy wept and laughed at the same time. "The question was, 'How many bubbles in a bar of soap?'"[3]

A week passed. It was Hector's lunch hour. He diagonally parked their Studebaker in front of the Voter Registration Office. Dorothy was church-dressed. A large tabby cat, happy as a carousel horse, pranced past them down the center of the empty street, then suddenly corkscrewed after a fly. A donkey placidly grazing across the street swiveled an ear toward them. "I'll wait here," he said, and squeezed her hand. "Don't worry. I'm proud of what you're doing, no matter what happens."

Before opening the door, Dorothy looked down at the green fringe between the sidewalk and the building wall and ob-

---

3. John Lewis, a civil rights leader, said in 2005, in a Democratic Radio Address on the fortieth anniversary of the Voting Rights Act, "Just forty years ago in many parts of the American South, it was almost impossible for people of color to register to vote. People stood day after day in unmovable lines waiting on the courthouse steps trying to register to vote. Doctors, lawyers, college professors, business owners, teachers, farmers, housewives, they all tried for years to pass the so-called literacy test. They were told they could not read or write well enough to pass the test. There was one man who had a Ph.D. degree, and he was asked how many bubbles there were in a bar of soap . . . People were beaten, taken to jail, and even killed trying to register to vote."

served that there were now many flowers, larger than before, exquisite bursts of red, orange, purple, and blue. Seeing these flowers calmed and somehow reassured her. She once again entered the Voter Registration Office and walked through the hallowed light to the counter, where the same clerk sat smoking. No hello. No excuse me. Dorothy simply quoted the Fifteenth Amendment to the United States Constitution that was added at the end of the Civil War: *"The right of citizens of the United States to vote shall not be denied or abridged by the United States or by any state on account of race, color, or previous condition of servitude."* Then she said, "I'm here to register to vote."

The woman behind the counter angrily said, "Girl, you have got some nerve. Don't you know your place?" A pause. She tapped her fingers. "Fill out this form."

"My name is Mrs. Milton. Is it 'How many bubbles in a bar of soap' again?"

"No, ma'am. Just fill out the form."

Dorothy sat down with the form, this time the same one given to white applicants, and filled in her name, age, address, profession, phone number, and Social Security number. There were no questions to answer this time. She brought it back to the counter.

"Thank you. That will be five dollars."

"FIVE DOLLARS?"

"Yes, it's a poll tax[4] of five dollars." The woman behind the

---

4. Actually, the poll tax was eliminated in early 1964. (But I took some liberty to illustrate the kinds of obstacles that voting officials threw in the

counter looked triumphant. "It must be paid before you can vote."

Dorothy glowered. "I don't have five dollars on me and we don't have five dollars to spare. And why should I have to pay to vote? Only rich folk can vote?"

"I'm sorry, ma'am, but that's the price."

"I'll be back," she muttered.

And once again Dorothy stalked out of the Voter Registration Office.

She and Hector drove home silently. Hector returned to work. She entered her kitchen and watered her flowers. She drank a cup of tea made from her own garden's mint. She sat and rocked. Then she picked up the phone and called the Southern Christian Leadership Conference, SCLC, in Atlanta, founded and directed by the Reverend Martin Luther King Jr. She spoke to the person on the other end of the line for at least an hour and a half.

---

way of blacks who wished to vote.) Blacks, with rare exception, were poor, and the poll tax of two to five dollars was more than most of them could afford. It was eliminated by 1) the XXIV Amendment to the Constitution, adopted in 1964, which said: "*Section 1.* The right of citizens of the United States to vote in any primary or other election for President or Vice President, for electors for President or Vice President, or for Senator or Representative in Congress, shall not be denied or abridged by the United States or any state by reason of failure to pay any poll tax or other tax. *Section 2.* The Congress shall have power to enforce this article by appropriate legislation"; 2) *Harper v. Virginia State Board of Elections*, decided in 1966 by the Supreme Court, abolished poll taxes for all other elections (for example mayors, dogcatchers, etc.).

Hector came home; they ate. Later that night, as they lay in bed reading, rain lightly strumming on their windows, the phone rang and Hector picked it up. He gravely listened for a moment and said, "I see." He hung up.

"Who was it?" Dorothy asked.

"Decker. I'm fired."

# V

Heidi, our boxer, and I waited at the bench in front of the Christian Science church halfway between our home and the Long Island Rail Road station. The sunset, filtered through a level-five pollution alert, was melted crayons. On time, my father walked toward me, briefcase in one hand, newspaper in the other. He attempted to read the paper as he walked. He looked up at the sunset, saw me, smiled, and I ran, grabbed his briefcase from him, and we walked home together. Heidi yanked us forward. His briefcase buckle came undone and I rebuckled it.

"Did you get me any pistachio nuts?" I asked.

"Not this time," he said.

"Ah, Dad."

"Sometime soon," he said. "For a special day."

As we walked, he flipped through the paper as though he was looking for something and not finding it.

After dinner, dishes, and homework, we made our way, one by one, into my mother and father's bedroom. And soon, like an open-face sandwich, our entire family, including Heidi, lay on their king bed. My mother, hair in curlers, read and marked student papers from her advanced high school Shakespeare class and ate Fiddle Faddle gourmet popcorn. She occasionally fed a piece to Heidi, who lay Sphinx-like beside her and watched her hand move between the box and her mouth with intense concentration. Now and then Heidi snapped at my mother's hand, but Mom, though intent on reading, was always too quick for her and pulled away in time. Occasionally my mom would read aloud a sentence or paragraph she liked. My dad, in a seersucker bathrobe, lay parallel to my mom, legal papers pancaked on top of him, some of them tumbling onto the floor. These were like the typed book reports that Josiah wrote, but thicker, on longer paper. He had circled words and sentences in blue pencil and was busily writing in the margins. Though *Batman* was on the TV, he effortlessly focused on his work.

He looked over at my mom. "Don't forget, we have to catch the seven o'clock news. It should be on."

"Okay," she said.

"What will be on?" I asked.

"You'll see," my father said.

"No, what?"

Josiah, "What?"

"You'll see. This has to do with my work. And I want you to see it. It's important. But not a word before it comes on."

I lay between my mother and father, Miracle-Combing my hair. Though curious about what my dad had said, I returned to *Popular Science* ("Scientists Describe Hostile Life on Venus"), watched Batman and Robin battle the Joker, and snuck Fiddle Faddle. Ezra and Josiah lay crossways at the foot of the bed. Ezra watched *Batman* as keenly as Heidi watched Fiddle Faddle while he dutifully rubbed my mother's toes, sore from her high heels. Josiah zinged a Slinky.

My mother checked her watch, then returned to her paper and chuckled. "Here, read this," she said, handing a student paper to my dad.

He read where she pointed and smiled. "He'll make a good lawyer someday," he said, checking his own watch.

Josiah beckoned with his fingers. She gave the paper to him and he snorted.

"Let me see," I said.

My mother showed me a sentence: *We must remember that all of the Shakespeare we read today is in translation.*

"What's so funny?" I asked. "That seems smart."

"Idiot," Josiah said. "Shakespeare was English and he wrote in English."

I thought a moment. "Old English," I said. "And you're a cretin."

"Old English," Josiah said, "is basically the same as English. Old English, my arse." He flicked me with his Slinky.

Ezra, the unobtrusive listener, seriously asked, "Is arse the same as ass?"

Josiah zinged me again and I kicked back. Heidi started running circles on top of all of us.

"Jack, do something."

My father did not look up from his papers.

"JACK, DO SOMETHING!"

My father scribbled on his paper a moment more, then looked up and surveyed Josiah and me with mild disgust. He checked the clock on the nightstand beside him.

"Josiah, turn it to the news."

"You turn it to the news."

My father tapped his palm on his forehead in mock pain, and looked upward in mock appeal to heaven.

But my mother locked her eyes on Josiah, and though his back was to her, he could still feel the heat from her lasers. He reluctantly turned to face her. She held up her hand and snapped her fingers. And Josiah got up and switched to the channel.

An announcer said, "This is the *CBS Evening News with Walter Cronkite.*" My father and mother sat up in bed and watched intently. By sympathetic vibration, my brothers and I sat up and watched, too. Walter Cronkite spoke in a voice as deep and rich and gravelly as granulated Ovaltine. "Good evening. Today in the news, Norwegian and Japanese Whaling Commission members, in defiance of other Western European and American commission members, have stated that they will continue to hunt the endangered minke whale. Demonstrators outside of commission headquarters protested and scuffles broke out with police. Nationally, continued drought in the Southwest has officials concerned and is driving up prices on the Chicago commodities market, adding to inflationary pressures. And President Johnson stood by the first lady as she announced the Highway Beautification Act, her plan to help beautify America by eliminating billboard clutter along our interstate highway system. More on all of this as our program continues."

My mother looked at my father, who was staring at the TV aghast. "Maybe it's about to come on," she said.

My father shook his head. "We'll see," he said.

"What will come on?" Josiah asked.

"Hold on," he said. "Either you'll find out, or I'll tell you when the program is over." And we watched the news, which elaborated on Cronkite's main points, reviewed the weather, and ended half an hour later.

"Okay, now tell us," Josiah said.

My father stared at the TV a moment more as if in disbelief. "Please turn it off," he said to Josiah. He looked over a moment at my mom, who clucked sympathetically, and then he turned to us.

"Today, in Selma, Alabama," he said, "a very important event in the struggle for civil rights took place. Martin Luther King and his followers demonstrated outside the Voter Registration Office to call attention to the outrageous, unfair, often violent tactics used there to prevent Negroes from registering to vote. If Negroes can't vote, then there is no possibility of peaceful change for the better. If there isn't peaceful change, there certainly will be violent change. So this is vital. Police arrested the whole lot of them, beating some so badly they ended up in the hospital. A man was shot by police and may die. They even arrested Negro schoolchildren!"

"Why did they beat them?" I asked. "Did they fight back when police tried to arrest them?"

"No," my father said. "King and his followers emphatically believe in a policy of nonviolence. They refuse to fight, even in self-defense. The police were just mean, vindictive."

"That's stupid," Josiah said. "Look what's happening in Vietnam. The government is forcing people to fight in an unjust war. And if they use force against citizens, why is it wrong to use force back?"

"Actually," my father said, "King is brilliant. He uses the tactics developed by Mahatma Gandhi in India's struggle for independence from the British. The British jailed and killed countless Indians, but the nonviolent response of Indians led by Gandhi clearly established their moral superiority. The British were seen by the world as cruel oppressors and eventually, under the pressure of world opinion, they were forced to leave India. Nonviolence trumped violence. But the problem is, if the media doesn't report on King, public opinion can't form in his favor."

"Dad, why don't you go to Selma and argue in court that it's illegal to prevent Negroes from voting?" I asked.

"It *is* illegal. Their right to vote is guaranteed by the Fifteenth Amendment to the United States Constitution. And the NAACP Legal Defense Fund has tried," he said. "But the judge in Selma, Daniel Thomas, is a flat-out racist. He has jurisdiction in Selma, and he will not do anything to prohibit illegal practices of the Voter Registration Office."

My father got up and flipped the channels for some time, but nothing about Selma was reported. He sat back down in bed; my mother took his hand. "Our lawyers are getting King and all the rest released from jail by tomorrow." My mother was about to respond when Heidi, whose only interest all along had been the Fiddle Faddle, grabbed the box and hightailed it from the room, Ezra in hot pursuit.

# VI

## The First Attempt to March

The Reverend Martin Luther King Jr. and his senior associates, Hosea Williams and John Lewis—long-serving, trusted colleagues—sat at Dorothy and Hector Milton's kitchen table, their Selma command center. Williams was a charismatic leader, unhesitating in the face of challenge, capable of firing up a crowd. Lewis was thoughtful, logical, focused, and brave, capable of marching into danger without histrionics.[1]

Drinking tea, eating grilled grouper, cheese grits, and turnip greens with little bits of bacon, they discussed strategy.

---

1. Actually, King had many associates in addition to Lewis and Williams—Ralph Abernathy, Jesse Jackson, Andrew Young, to name just a few. However, because Lewis and Williams were particularly central to events I describe, I focus on them.

The perfume of Dorothy's indoor garden was so luxuriant it had a texture, like a silk scarf pulled slowly across your face.

"The problem is," said Williams, "that we have not called attention to ourselves or our cause. Greenberg and his Legal Defense Fund team got us out of jail, but people are focused on the Vietnam War and on Japanese whales and have no attention to spare for our troubles. Not a single national newspaper or television station covered our demonstration."

"If you keep eating those cheese grits like that," said Lewis, "you're going to be a Japanese whale and then we'll get some attention." Everyone laughed.

Dorothy, a daisy blossom in her hair, spooned more cheese grits onto everyone's plates and poured more chilled, sweetened mint tea.

"The question is," said Lewis, "what can we do to bring attention to our plight? Malcolm X is gaining sway with more of our people. He just arrived in town. Says we must meet violence with violence. Some of our folk are becoming impatient for change. They just might start believing him. We must do something to head this off and we must do it soon."

King sat back, sipped his tea, and listened to his associates. "The grouper is delicious," he said to Dorothy. "Where did you get it?"

"My daughter's husband, Obadiah, caught it very early this morning out of Mobile and, knowing you were here and how you liked it, drove it up on ice. There's more."

"No, thank you. I don't seek to be harpooned like Hosea here." Then, seriously, "We must march, many of us must march, from Selma to Montgomery, the state capital. A major demonstration like this, with the press invited, is what's required to advertise our situation and influence public opinion."[2]

"That's right," said Hector, who sat on the far side of the kitchen working over sheets of newspaper on an irrigation-pump carburetor. Since getting fired from Gallagher's, he had been doing small-engine repairs.

King looked at Hector and smiled. "How's business going?" he asked.

"Well, sir, I would not say that business is as frisky as a Morgan horse in a barley patch, but yet again it's not as slow as cold molasses. It goes."

King grinned and turned back to Lewis and Williams. "We will march from the Edmund Pettus Bridge, on the outskirts of Selma here, to Montgomery, the capital of Alabama, where I will give a speech, directed to Governor George Wallace, seeking redress of our grievances."

Williams and Lewis both spoke at the same time, Williams riding over Lewis. "There will be hell to pay, sir. You know Governor Wallace's favorite phrase: *'Segregation now, segregation tomorrow, and segregation forever'.*[3] There is no way he will allow you to march. We will have to do so illegally. And

---

2. I have simplified considerably here. King didn't conceive of this course of action during one meeting. In fact, the plan originated with one of King's executive aides, James Bevel.

3. Wallace spoke these words at his 1963 inauguration as governor of Alabama.

if we break the law, that will bring a confrontation, probably a violent one, with the police."

"Protest, nonviolent protest, is our most important card to play, the only moral card, and we must play it, despite the cost," said King. "Now, let's schedule a date for the march and I'll leave it to the two of you to exercise your considerable talents and arrange the logistics. And this time let's be very certain that the newspapers and television stations know the date and location of our protest way in advance."

All three men got out their calendars and discussed dates. Finally, Sunday, March 7, was agreed upon, and they parted, King to rejoin them on the sixth.

Months passed and John Lewis and Hosea Williams did exercise their considerable talents to arrange the logistics of the march. And when King had not arrived from Atlanta on the sixth, they called.

"Oh Lord," said King. "Oh Lord. The march is tomorrow? You won't believe this, but I marked it on my pocket calendar for next Sunday, the fourteenth, and it is impossible for me to make it to Selma in time. Is rescheduling the march a possibility?"

"No, sir," said Lewis and Williams at the same time, each on different phone extensions. "The horses are straining at the gate."

"If we cancel," said Lewis, "I don't know what our people may do. They may even riot. It's possible."

"I feel we have to go ahead with this," said Williams.

"Sir, I agree," said Lewis. "Governor George Wallace has

forbidden our march. And we must make the point now that we will not let him intimidate us."

"All right," said King. "You must explain to everyone that this is my mistake and I take full responsibility for it. The two of you will lead. I will follow your situation closely from Atlanta. And remember above all there must, there absolutely must be no violence. We can only hold the moral high ground if we remain nonviolent no matter what provocation. Otherwise we will be perceived in exactly the same light as the Klan and Wallace and his goons. Only if we demonstrate peacefully will we exert pressure to put an end to the injustice our people suffer. This is critical. If you run into trouble, and obviously there is a high chance you will, immediately contact Greenberg to get the Legal Defense Fund on board, is this understood?"

"Understood," said Williams and Lewis.

"God bless," said King.

And so on the morning of March 7, 1965, a day that would be known forever after as "Bloody Sunday," John Lewis and Hosea Williams stood on the Selma side of the Edmund Pettus Bridge—a bridge that looked as if it had been built from an Erector set—with five hundred followers behind them, mainly black men, though some black women could not be kept away. This included Hector Milton and Dorothy, who wore a flowered wool scarf. The road they stood upon was nubbly, patched with tar, unfriendly to shoes. The morning was cold and vapor appeared at every breath.

All along the shoulder of the road were cameramen and journalists from every major national television station and newspaper. Lewis and Williams had informed them well in advance. They keenly watched the proceedings, checked focus on their cameras, jotted in their notebooks. They could feel the tension like a massive spring overwound.

In a line directly in front of the marchers, blocking the bridge, stood a phalanx of state troopers, led by Major John Cloud. Bulky gas masks dangled from their belts.

The troopers looked to Cloud. Some were nervous. Others smiled or chuckled. One with an aluminum front tooth pressed his finger to a nostril and blew his nose directly onto the asphalt. Another licked his lips with a dry tongue, as lizards do.

Hosea Williams and John Lewis looked at each other.[4] Williams whispered to Lewis, "Can you swim?"

"No," said Lewis.

"I can't either," said Williams, "and I'm sure we're gonna end up in that river."

John Lewis approached Cloud. "May I have a word with you, Major?"

"There is no word to be had," Cloud replied. "You have two minutes to disperse." He started counting.

"Sir—" said Lewis, but he was cut off.

"Advance!" called Major Cloud, and his troopers shoved into the crowd of marchers, hitting them with their billy clubs. Troopers threw tear gas and nausea gas at the marchers. There was screaming, crying, retching, running, confusion. Many marchers collapsed in pools of blood.

---

4. This dialogue is taken from the nonfiction account of events in the book *Selma, 1965*, by Charles Fager.

All of a sudden Cloud's troopers were joined by Sheriff James Clark and his "squirrel shooters," two hundred local possemen deputized for the occasion, many on horseback.

Clark wore a white helmet. On his tailored uniform was a button that said NEVER (Governor Wallace's one word slogan against integration). On one hip was a gun, on the other a nightstick. He shouted, "Get the niggers!"

Possemen on horseback ran over marchers, the horse hooves breaking bones, cracking skulls. In some cases, a deputy ran over a marcher, then wheeled his horse and did it again and again and again. One marcher cut across the road and sprinted into a garage. A deputy chased him into the garage on his horse, sparks snapping from its hooves, and then struck him on the head with a club, knocking him senseless. Another marcher ran into the First Baptist Church and was followed by possemen, who grabbed him and threw him through a stained-glass window portraying Jesus the Good Shepherd.

Possemen banged their nightsticks on cars and hollered, "We want all niggers off the streets!" *Bang, bang, bang.*

Many marchers knelt and prayed, and possemen hit them with clubs made from rubber tubing wrapped in barbed wire, ripping open their skin, tearing open their scalps. Or they were struck with bullwhips that shredded their shirts and pants and slashed the skin from their backs. Local white bystanders cheered. Not a single marcher fought back.

All of this was captured by still cameras and television cameras. Reporters took notes.

Almost every demonstrator was arrested and taken to jail

or, if badly injured, the hospital. Of course, they were brought to the "Coloreds" section of the jail and the "Coloreds" section of the hospital. Before entering the hospital with a skull fracture, John Lewis spoke to remaining marchers. *"I don't see how President Johnson can send troops to Vietnam . . . and he can't send troops to Selma, Alabama. Next time we march, we may have to keep going when we get to Montgomery. We may have to go on to Washington."*

Jack Greenberg got the call. Lawyers of the NAACP Legal Defense Fund soon arrived to help free those arrested.

By then the highway on the Selma side of the Edmund Pettus Bridge was empty, except for bloodstains, empty tear-gas canisters, clods of horse manure, and film containers discarded by photographers and cameramen. And, beneath a detached horseshoe, a flowered scarf.

# VII

I walked home from school and stopped, not far from the train station, at Beverly Bakery, for cookie samples. Their cookies were delicious, buttery and slightly chewy. If you asked nicely, the lady behind the counter, who was born a grandmother, would give you a bit of broken cookie from that day's baking.

"May I have a cookie, please?"

She smiled, reached below the cash register, and sweetly handed me half an oatmeal-raisin cookie from a red plastic tray mounded with broken cookies. "I love a child who says 'please' and 'thank you,'" she said. "'Please' and 'thank you' are very important. More children should learn this." The lady had a slight accent.

"Thank you," I said, and stepped outside and sat down on a bench to eat it.

One of the school's black students walked up to me and said, "Do they really give out free cookies in there?"

"You bet they do," I said, feeling generous with something that wasn't mine. "Every day. They've got lots behind the counter on a tray. Just ask the lady inside. She's nice."

"Great," he said, and went in.

A moment later he came out empty-handed and puzzled. "Guess they ran out," he said, and walked off.

I was puzzled, too, but quickly forgot it and walked the rest of the way home.

My dad came home early, at four-thirty. I met him at the station and we walked home.

"Any pistachios?"

"Nope, not yet."

We passed Beverly Bakery. "Just a sec," I said, and, having forgotten they'd run out, stepped in for another broken cookie.

"Velcome back," said the lady behind the counter, bobbling her $v$'s and $w$'s. "Vhat a sweet tooth you have."

"May I have a cookie, please?"

She pulled forth the cookie tray and handed me another half cookie, this time chocolate chip. I thanked her and rejoined my dad. I flashed back to the black student who got no cookie. Could that woman be a racist? No, not possible. Yet, they hadn't run out of cookies. I was scared of the blacks in the projects. Was I a racist? Malcolm X hated me. Was he a racist? I had a faint sense of powerful electric currents flowing around me and no longer felt protected. I lost my appetite and I dropped the cookie in a trash can. My dad was the perfect insulator, though, and I walked home comfortable in his presence. As we walked, he read the paper at the same time. Clearly he was excited, because he actually slapped the paper.

"What?" I said.

"Tonight you'll see it on TV for sure, you just wait. Today is a day of change." With rare emotion he said it again, "Today is a day of change."

After dinner, dishes, and homework, all of us piled back on my parents' bed for the *CBS Evening News with Walter Cronkite*.

"Good evening. Today in Selma, Alabama, peaceful Negro demonstrators attempting to march in protest against voter discrimination were viciously attacked by the local police."

There was footage of state troopers firing gas at protesters who doubled over coughing and retching, of Major Cloud's troopers and James Clark and his possemen whipping and clubbing protesters who knelt and prayed. The camera focused on a deputy whose horse repeatedly kicked an obviously unconscious protester. The deputy laughed. In another shot, a policeman punched a woman, who wore a scarf, in the face. Not a single protester fought back.

Ezra whimpered. Josiah started pacing back and forth. My heart pounded. My mother whispered, "God, Jack. God."

"These American citizens, many of whom defended us in

World War Two," continued Cronkite, "were protesting the unfair and illegal tactics used by the Selma Voter Registration Office to prevent Negroes from voting. Those Negroes who attempt to register to vote are given fraudulent tests, are threatened, and often attacked. When President Johnson was asked about this at his weekly press conference this afternoon, he said, *'I am certain Americans everywhere join in deploring the brutality with which a number of Negro citizens of Alabama were treated when they sought to dramatize their deep and sincere interest in attaining the precious right to vote.'"*

The phone rang. My mother picked it up. "Phyllis Sutherd," she mouthed to my father. "Yes," she said, "yes," and "yes" once more, then hung up. She turned to my father. "She's very upset. She wants you to do something."

The phone rang again, and I picked it up. "Duvy mon, is your mapa there?"

"Yes," I said to Sally, our housekeeper.

"Well, tell them I won't be comin' ta work tomorr. People here be ver' upset, mon, upset most outrageous, and I doona think it be safe for me to. The streets be totally agitated. But I believe I be comin' next week after, God be will."

"Okay," I said, and relayed her message as best I understood it to my parents.

The phone rang again. "Hello," a voice said.

"Hello."

"Are you Josiah?"

"No. David."

"David, the middle son?"

"Yes."

"Your father tells me that you're very talented."

"At what?" I asked.

"Words."

Good at words. What an odd conversation. Who was I talking to? The voice was strangely familiar, obviously Southern and almost melodious, but I couldn't place it.

"And how is your mother?"

"She's fine."

"Good. May I speak with your father?"

Feeling formal all of a sudden, I asked, "Who may I say is calling?"

"His good friend Martin."

I gulped. "Phone call for you, Dad. Martin Luther King."

All of us stared at my father.

"Jack," said King, "did you see it?"

"Yes, I did," said my father. "Our lawyers are there right now, working for everyone's release."

"John's in the hospital with a fractured skull."

"I didn't know that," my father said. "That's awful. Will he be okay?"

"We hope so," said King. "We hope."

"We're doing all we can," said my father.

"I know you are, Jack. But, from the strategic point of view, how do you see it?"

"We have to get an injunction against the sheriff and his men to prevent them from interfering with another attempt to march. But the problem is that Thomas won't follow the law.

We have to find a way to get the case before Frank Johnson in Montgomery. Johnson is sympathetic to our cause and he has the guts to do something about it. So Montgomery is the key."

"Thank you, Jack. You see it much as I see it. We'll talk later."

Josiah took a deep breath, shaking with emotion, and stared at our father.

# VIII

## President Lyndon Johnson Responds

The large red pumper truck snouted from the garage and pulled onto the White House back lawn, standard procedure whenever Marine One, President Johnson's personal helicopter, took off or landed. Firemen connected one hose to a pressurized tank of chemical fire retardant and another to a yellow fire hydrant, and stood tensely, ready to deal with any possible emergency. In front of the White House gates, crowds protesting the Vietnam War were joined by a small group of demonstrators waving placards, chanting, and angrily shouting about the lack of government response to the violence in Selma. The Secret Service agents were very much on edge. The number of sniper patrols on the White House roof had been doubled and the dust filters on Marine One's turbines had been removed in order to let them gulp more air for greater power and speed if required.

The helicopter blades spun faster and faster until they were a blur. At the last possible moment, when they were up to takeoff speed, President Johnson, his wife, Lady Bird, and his top aide, Clark Clifford, were quickly bundled aboard by Secret Service, and the chopper arced upward. Two armed military choppers followed at a short distance, decoys in case of ground fire. They were on their way to Camp David, the President's country retreat. The President could see the demonstrators below, shaking their fists angrily at his helicopter. At him. He could barely make out a sign one was waving up at him: LBJ, JUST YOU WAIT . . . SEE WHAT HAPPENS IN '68. He hated being hated.

A handsome Marine steward, wearing a perfectly creased, full military uniform, including a Bronze Medal for valor in combat and a Purple Heart for shrapnel wounds, asked the passengers if they would like a drink or snack.

"The usual on the rocks for me, Caras, and some of those fancy cheesies we served the Italian ambassador, or was it their prime minister?" said Johnson. "Or maybe it was the Venezuelan president," he muttered to himself. He leaned back in his seat, closed his eyes, and put his forehead against the bulletproof window to chill his headache. Lady Bird Johnson and Clifford took drinks in frosted glasses. The vibration was uncomfortable against Johnson's head and he sat up straight. "What do you think we should do about this nigra King and his demonstrators in Selma?" he asked Clifford.

"As you know, much of your support for Vietnam comes

from the South," said Clifford. "The Southern states are absolutely dead set against making any concession to King and his people. They are perceived as rabble-rousers who want to destroy the set order of things. Give them an inch and they'll take a mile. Next thing you know, Negro men will be dating their daughters. You don't want to alienate the Southern states."

Johnson loosened his seat belt, leaned forward, and put his hands on his knees.

"On the other hand," said Clifford, "demonstrations are erupting across the country in support of King. Everyone saw the police attack peaceful demonstrators. Here, read this telegram from Jackie Robinson. He's a hero to all baseball fans, Negro and white. It sums things up perfectly." And Clifford handed Johnson a Western Union envelope.

**IMPORTANT YOU TAKE IMMEDIATE ACTION IN ALABAMA. ONE MORE DAY OF SAVAGE TREATMENT BY LEGALIZED HATCHET MEN COULD LEAD TO OPEN WARFARE BY AROUSED NEGROES. AMERICA CANNOT AFFORD THIS IN 1965.**

"Hmm," said Johnson. "So, either way I'm screwed."

"Lyndon," said his wife, "do what's right. Forget the political calculations and do what's right."[1]

---

1. President Johnson's wife, Claudia Taylor, known to most as Lady Bird, came from an affluent family in Texas. She supported civil rights and was deeply committed to helping the underprivileged. For instance, as part of her husband's War on Poverty, Lady Bird promoted the Head Start Program, designed to help poor, preschool children improve their learning skills.

The steward, Lieutenant Moody Caras, whose wounds ached as the air pressure dropped, echoed her under his breath, "Do what's right."

"You know," said Johnson, "since Lincoln freed the slaves, I have done more for the nigras of this nation than any other president. And they do not appreciate me for it. They do not appreciate me."[2] He paused, ruminated. "And if I support King, it may require federal troops, and if I bring in federal troops, we may have open warfare in the streets. And that may set back the civil rights movement for years."

"Sir," said Clifford, "it's a tough call, but in my opinion your smartest course here, notwithstanding all your concerns, is to do what you know is right. You want history to remember you as the person who fought racism, who stood up for the oppressed, not the opposite. You want to prevent riots. With the country divided over Vietnam, that's the last thing we need."

President Johnson thought momentarily of his hardscrabble childhood in Texas, he thought of the endless bad news from Vietnam, he thought of riots in which whites and Negroes would hatefully call out against him, and made a quick calculation. "Write a forceful, eloquent paper for me that I can read on national television in complete support of King and his nigras. We will take the high road on this one and leave behind those who don't."

---

2. The Civil Rights Act of 1964, introduced by Kennedy but passed during Johnson's tenure, required nondiscrimination in public accommodations, employment, and all federally funded activity.

# IX

From our usual spots on our parents' bed, we all watched President Johnson's special address to Congress. He stepped to the podium, a place from which wars had been declared and peace counseled. A podium steeped in history. And, speaking with force and dignity, he proposed the 1965 Voting Rights Act.

> *I speak tonight for the dignity of man and the*
> *destiny of Democracy. I urge every member of both*
> *parties, Americans of all religions and of all colors,*
> *from every section of this country, to join me in*
> *that cause.*
> *At times history and fate meet at a single time*
> *in a single place to shape a turning point in man's*

*unending search for freedom. So it was at Lexington*
*and Concord. So it was a century ago at Appomattox.*
*So it was last week in Selma, Alabama. There, long*
*suffering men and women peacefully protested the*
*denial of their rights as Americans. Many of them*
*were brutally assaulted . . .*

*. . . Rarely in any time does an issue lay bare the*
*secret heart of America itself. Rarely are we met with*
*a challenge, not to our growth or abundance, or our*
*welfare or our security, but rather to the values and*
*the purposes and the meaning of our beloved nation.*
*The issue of equal rights for American Negroes is*
*such an issue. And should we defeat every enemy,*
*and should we double our wealth and conquer the*
*stars, and still be unequal to this issue, then we will*
*have failed as a people and as a nation. For, with a*
*country as with a person, "what is a man profited if*
*he shall gain the whole world, and lose his own soul?"*

*There is no Negro problem. There is no Southern*
*problem. There is no Northern problem. There is*
*only an American problem . . . And we are met*
*here tonight as Americans—not as Democrats or*
*Republicans; we're met here as Americans to solve*
*that problem . . .*

*Many of the issues of civil rights are very complex*
*and most difficult. But about this there can and*
*should be no argument. Every American citizen must*
*have an equal right to vote. There is no reason which*

can excuse the denial of that right. There is no duty which weighs more heavily on us than the duty we have to insure that right. Yet the harsh fact is that in many places in this country, men and women are kept from voting simply because they are Negroes.

Every device of which human ingenuity is capable has been used to deny this right. The Negro citizen may go to register only to be told that the day is wrong, or the hour is late, or the official in charge is absent. And if he persists and, if he manages to present himself to the registrar, he may be disqualified because he did not spell out his middle name, or because he abbreviated a word on the application. And if he manages to fill out an application, he is given a test. The registrar is the sole judge of whether he passes this test. He may be asked to recite the entire Constitution, or explain the most complex provisions of state law.

And even a college degree cannot be used to prove that he can read and write. For the fact is that the only way to pass these barriers is to show a white skin. Experience has clearly shown that the existing process of law cannot overcome systematic and ingenious discrimination. No law that we now have on the books . . . can insure the right to vote when local officials are determined to deny it. In such a case, our duty must be clear to all of us. The

*Constitution says that no person shall be kept from voting because of his race or his color.*

*We have all sworn an oath before God to support and to defend that Constitution. We must now act in obedience to that oath. Wednesday, I will send to Congress a law designed to eliminate illegal barriers to the right to vote . . . This bill will establish a simple, uniform standard which cannot be used, however ingenious the effort, to flout our Constitution. It will provide for citizens to be registered by officials of the United States Government, if the state officials refuse to register them . . .*

*There is no Constitutional issue here. The command of the Constitution is plain. There is no moral issue. It is wrong—deadly wrong—to deny any of your fellow Americans the right to vote in this country.*

*But even if we pass this bill the battle will not be over. What happened in Selma is part of a far larger movement which reaches into every section and state of America. It is the effort of American Negroes to secure for themselves the full blessings of American life. Their cause must be our cause too. Because it's not just Negroes, but really it's all of us, who must overcome the crippling legacy of bigotry and injustice.*

And then President Johnson paused, looked out at his audience, slowly raised his arms above his head, and, echoing the anthem of Martin Luther King's rallies, said, *"And We Shall Overcome."*

The audience, mainly congressmen and senators, was silent for a moment, and then spontaneously rose and burst into cheers and wild applause, stamping their feet. Grown men and women, both in the audience and watching the speech on television, sobbed.

Johnson went on, harking back to his early years as a schoolteacher, adding:

> *My first job after college was as a teacher in*
> *Cotulla, Texas, in a small Mexican-American school.*
> *Few of them could speak English, and I couldn't*
> *speak much Spanish. My students were poor and*
> *they often came to class without breakfast, hungry.*
> *They knew even in their youth the pain of prejudice.*
> *They never seemed to know why people disliked*
> *them. But they knew it was so, because I saw it in*
> *their eyes. I often walked home late in the afternoon,*
> *after the classes were finished, wishing there was*
> *more that I could do. But all I knew was to teach*
> *them the little that I knew, hoping that it might help*
> *them against the hardships that lay ahead.*
>
> *Somehow you never forget what poverty and*
> *hatred can do when you see its scars on the hopeful*
> *face of a young child.*

*I never thought then, in 1928, that I would be*
*standing here in 1965. It never even occurred to me*
*in my fondest dreams that I might have the chance to*
*help the sons and daughters of those students and to*
*help people like them all over this country.*

*But now I do have that chance—and I'll let you*
*in on a secret—I mean to use it. And I hope that you*
*will use it with me.*

And people sobbed again.

"So the problem in Selma is solved," said Josiah, wiping his eyes. "The President has spoken and racist tricks are now against the law."

"Unfortunately not," said my father. "This is an extremely important step. But in order for the Voting Rights Act to become law, it must be enacted by Congress. And many in Congress are from Southern states or states on the Southern fringe, and they are against or unsympathetic to Negro rights. Things hang in the balance. And enough public pressure must be brought to bear to swing things our way. The problem is that if they march, they'll all be arrested again, and they need the publicity that a long march will bring, not just the publicity of being beaten. George Wallace, the governor of Alabama, has issued an order saying they may not march. However, there is a federal judge in Montgomery, Frank Johnson, who can override the governor's order. If King wants to march again, he can only do so if Judge Johnson prohibits Wallace, Sheriff Clark, and their gang from breaking up the march. Tonight we're preparing the papers at the office and in the morning I will fly to Montgomery with Legal Defense Fund lawyers to file the case."

"Will you win?" I asked.

"I think there's a good chance I will. Frank Johnson was one of the judges who ruled in favor of Rosa Parks."

"Who's Rosa Parks?" I asked.

My father looked at me in disbelief.

And then Ezra, eight years old, usually silent, spoke up, though directing his comments to Heidi. "Rosa Parks is the Negro woman who refused to give up her bus seat to a white passenger even though the law said she had to."

Both my father and I tilted our heads at Ezra, astonished.

"Where did you learn that?" my father asked, chuckling, shaking his head.

"From Duvy's *Weekly Reader*," Ezra said, still addressing Heidi, then nuzzling her snout.

"Well, you're right," my father said, smiling. "And after the decision, the Ku Klux Klan was so angry they burned a cross on Judge Johnson's lawn. They refer to him as 'the most hated man in Alabama' because of his decisions favoring justice for Negroes. He's courageous and that's why I believe he'll do the right thing."

I hung my head. This is something I should have known. This was important. I resolved to learn more. I looked at my little brother with newfound respect.

# X

## The Weight on King's Shoulders

Dorothy and Hector Milton's blue-tick hound watched as a neighbor's cat sauntered saucily along their roofline. The dog licked his lips. *I'll get him yet*, he thought. *No way*, smirked the cat. Finches warbled and the morning air was still cool and fragrant with night's exhalation. The yard was completely enclosed by a picket fence that took its job seriously in the manner of its owners, no slouching tolerated.

"I know it was just a misunderstanding," Hosea Williams said to King, "but there is talk, mainly among the hotheads, that you didn't march because you lacked the courage and conviction." The group sat around the breakfast table, drinking coffee and eating hush puppies, country ham, and eggs sunny-side up. The eggs were from Dorothy Johnson's Buttercup hens out back. Dorothy had a terrible black eye, only now turning the color of expired steak.

"How's your head?" King asked John.

"Headache," said Lewis.

King spoke quietly, yet rhythmically, with crisp enunciation. "Okay. Well then, they all should know that jail cells and I are not unacquainted. The problem, though, is that if we march and we're stopped and I get put in jail, that doesn't help our situation one bit. We need to march between Selma and Montgomery to show all Americans the immorality of trampling Negro rights. Only when this is crystal clear to them will they exert pressure on their congressmen to support President Johnson's Voting Rights Act. The key here is public opinion."

Dorothy refilled their coffee cups and King smiled at her. "Your breakfast is delicious, Dorothy, thank you. How is Hector this morning?"

Hector's collarbone had been cracked by a trooper's nightstick during the attempted march out of Selma. And he was upstairs in bed healing.

"He is, to use his own words, as jumpy as a flea in a pillowcase, or almost," she said. "I've had to order him to lie still. More eggs?"

"So that means," said John Lewis, "that we pin our hopes on the Legal Defense Fund and Jack Greenberg's team. He argues before Federal Judge Frank Johnson tomorrow. If Johnson doesn't grant permission to march, you will have two options. One, you will have to defy him and march. You'll be jailed and there may be riots, which will play into the hands of racist authorities. They'll say we're violent and uncivilized, proving that our organization and its goals are illegitimate. Or, two, you will have to obey him and not march, making it appear like you are buckling to the white establishment, and many of our people may desert us."

King shook his head, hoping his weariness didn't show. Heavy responsibility rested on his shoulders. There was so much pain and anger among his people and so many passionate, differing points of view about what should be done to bring justice. "Well, we'll just have to see what happens tomorrow."

# XI

My hair had to behave. The directions on the tube of Score hair gel said that just a little dab, the amount equivalent to what you'd use to brush your teeth, was enough for a head of hair. Not hair like mine. I put about ten times as much on my hand and rubbed it thoroughly into my hair. Then I took my Miracle Comb and attacked. Behold, my hair was straight at last, though an uninformed observer might have thought I'd shellacked my head with Vaseline. I looked with satisfaction. *Boing.* As though to taunt me, a curl slowly formed at the center of my forehead. *Boing. Boing.* I stared at my hair and waggled my finger in the mirror. "I'm not done with you yet."

A glorious morning polished by a night of shooting stars. Neighborhood children bicycled in the street, called out to one another, laughed. I ran outside to get the newest edition of *Popular Science*. I reached into the mailbox next to our pear tree and pulled out something on flimsy paper with smudged ink: *The Thunderbolt, Newspaper of the Ku Klux Klan*. There was a photo of my dad on the front page and the caption read: VICIOUS JEW JACK GREENBERG. I dropped the paper as if it were a poison spider. Then, heart stuttering, I picked it up again and read *Greenberg—Jewish lawyer from Jew York City—uses fancy language and lawyer tricks to help niggers (like Martin Luther Coon) get around the law. This may bring suffering to many innocent niggers or even to himself.*

I ran into the house, raced up the stairs, and skidded into my mom and dad's bedroom. My mother looked up with alarm. "What's this?" I asked her.

She barely looked at the paper and froze.

"What is it?" I insisted.

She cautiously took the paper from my hand and, as though it were used tissue, dropped it into the wastebasket. "It's a paper from the Ku Klux Klan. We've been getting them, and letters, too, for some time and I've been throwing them out. You just beat me to it this time." My mom was shaking slightly.

"But how did they get our address?"

"We don't know. The phone book, probably." My mom grabbed and hugged me. "There's nothing to worry about, sweetheart. Nothing at all."

I could feel her tears on my cheek. Then I heard her choke slightly, and she began crying so hard she couldn't breathe correctly. My shirt became wet with her tears.

"Mom, you're squeezing me too tight. Let go." She loosened her embrace. I looked at her face and yelped. Her mascara, blush, and even her lipstick were running, making her look like one of the face-painted Chinese Opera performers who had visited our school last week.

My mother's wailing and shaking increased. She started hiccuping and honking as she cried. Josiah looked in, rolled his eyes, withdrew. Ezra ran in, grabbed her leg, and said, "Mom, it's okay, it's okay, it's okay."

I echoed him. "It's okay, Mom, it's okay."

Eventually my mother's crying stopped and her breathing returned to normal, though occasionally her body would convulse. Heidi licked her shoe and looked up at her with concern.

"Are we in danger?" I asked. "Is that why you're crying?"

"Of course not," she quickly said. "I'm just moody today."

An hour later, we walked out to the station wagon, got in. We were going to my touch-football game. "Wait a minute," I said, and ran back into the house for a notebook and pen. When I returned to the car I heard on the radio, "In fighting by the Cambodian border supported by Marine helicopter brigades and light armor, the military reports thirty-four American soldiers have died, and four hundred and twenty-three Vietcong."

"Great," I said out loud, "we're winning."

"Are you crazy?" Josiah squeaked. "Are you completely crazy?"

"Whaddya mean, crazy? We're winning. We're ahead."

"You are crazy. What makes you think we're winning?"

"Because more of them have died than us."

"WHAT? You think if we just kill enough Vietcong we'll win?"

"Yes, why not?"

"Because you'd have to kill every person in Vietnam and China to win. And we don't even know for sure if it's Vietcong we're killing. Probably we're killing innocent civilians as well. If this war is going on when I reach draft age, I'm not going."

"That's right," my mother said.

"And beyond that," said Josiah, "proportionately, more Negroes are drafted and sent over there than whites, and more are killed than whites. It's racist."

Ezra said nothing, but solemnly stared forward as he drank from a family-size bottle of apple juice through a straw.

"Mom, doesn't he have to obey the law even if he doesn't like it?" I asked.

"No way," Josiah said. "I'd move to Canada."

And my mother, speaking in her high-school-English-teacher voice, all her words perfectly stitched with commas and periods, said, "It is a citizen's obligation to follow the law. However, if you deeply, seriously feel in your heart of hearts that the law is immoral, then your highest obligation is to what is right, not what is lawful. And this war is wrong. We are supporting a corrupt regime in Saigon. We are fighting to prevent a country from determining its own political fate, something we have no right to do and certainly something for which so many of our young men shouldn't die. How would you feel if the Chinese invaded us in order to force us to become Communists?"

I mulled this over. Were there any circumstances in which a person would be justified in breaking the law? Wasn't it the very nature of the law that even if you didn't like it, you had to obey it for the greater good? My mother was Authority and I didn't question her, not really, and it troubled me that she would question the Law, a greater authority yet.

We arrived at the park for my touch-football game. I gulped and my breathing quickened as I stepped out of the car and walked over to the field, notebook and pen in hand. "Words, correctly used, are extraordinarily powerful," I said to myself. None of the other players paid me any attention as I joined them. "And, after all," I repeated several times quickly, as though to make it true, "I'm talented at words."

Leo Jones seemed to look right through me while he discussed strategy with teammates. "I'll run straight out and hook left. John, Dan, you run straight out, clearing a path for Paul. Paul, you follow them and lateral the ball—"

"Excuse me, guys," I said.

Leo kept speaking: "—to me. Then I'll run up the sidelines and you do what you can to—"

"Just one thing, guys," I said.

"What is it, Greenberg?" Leo asked. "You're interrupting."

"You're right. I apologize. I just wanted you to know that I am writing an article about our team for the *Great Neck Record*." Eyes widened. "And I'm going to include information about every single one of you who wants to be interviewed."

Eyes widened more. Like iron filings attracted to a magnet, the density pattern of the group shifted somewhat from Leo to me.

"Interview me," said Dan Kozlarek.

"And me," said Jimmy Hackenger.

"And me," said Jeff Anik.

Paul Ferber looked between Leo and me. "And me, too," he said.

"Okay, guys," I replied with a confidence I didn't feel. "You play the game, and afterward I'll talk to you."

"Okay, Greenberg, after the game," said Paul. "By the way, what's with your hair?"

"I'm a juvenile delinquent, you know, a greaser," I said, joking.

"Oh," he said, not getting it.

Leo looked at me, perplexed, scanned my hair suspiciously, took up where he left off, and all of the iron filings shifted back to him.

Even though I didn't play, feigning a strained knee, we lost by a point. But this seemed to affect no one's spirits as they all (except for Leo) ran up to me following the game and I got a few facts from each. My plan was working! As I was leaving, Leo beckoned me with his finger. Wow, the team captain wanted to talk to me. Clearly I'd had a great idea. I walked over. Leo leaned to whisper. "Jerk," he said, and strode off.

My mom returned from errands to get me. On the drive home, Ezra, who sat up front next to his empty bottle of apple juice, said, "I have to pee."

"You can pee when we get home," my mother said.

"No, I have to pee now, really bad," Ezra said.

"Well, there's no place to stop here," my mother said, "so you have to pee in the bottle."

"Okay," he said without complaint.

Still brooding over Leo's remark, I heard a rustle from up front and all of a sudden I felt something warm on my arm. It took me a moment to realize it was wet. Perplexed, I focused forward and saw a golden stream of pee arcing back over Ezra's head from the front seat, falling directly onto me.

"AAAAAHHHHHH!" I screamed. "You're peeing on me!" I started banging Ezra on the head, and the pee, seemingly inexhaustible in supply, started streaming back and forth, still backward over his head, across the entire backseat. Josiah, beside me, started screaming and we both started hitting Ezra. And then the fire hose was loose! A fountain of pee lacquered the inside of the windshield, my mother, Josiah, and me. Heidi, who'd leaped into the backseat with us, jumped back and forth through it like a child through a sprinkler.

My mother began screaming and weaved the car down the road, onto the median, almost into oncoming traffic, back onto the median. Like a stunt driver, she steered the car at a sharp angle onto the shoulder. I thought I knew what she would say next: "Would you like to walk?!" But what she did was worse. She took off her shoe, twisted backward, and tried to bang us with it—not quite reaching, though. She was crying, and occasionally hiccuping with laughter. Her nose was running. And she said, "*I'm* walking."

She flung her door open, almost hitting a passing car, jumped out, and started gimping down the shoulder of the road one shoe on, one off. My brothers and I stayed in the car. I felt shocked, mortified, scared. Ezra was wailing.

"I can understand why she might be mad," Josiah said tensely. "But this is crazy."

I remembered how hard Mom cried when I'd shown her the Ku Klux Klan newspaper. And then Mrs. Sutherd's words— "stay safe"—popped into my mind again. And suddenly, like puzzle pieces coming together, I realized: Mom wasn't mad. She was worried. She was worried for Dad. In fact, she was scared out of her wits.

She returned to us. We drove silently home. We showered. We each scrounged our own dinner. Pop-Tarts for Josiah. Cocoa Puffs for Ezra. Campbell's Tomato Soup and a glass of sherry for Mom. I made spaghetti with a sauce of heavy cream and fresh-squeezed lemon juice (simmered in a saucepan until syrupy) with fried bread crumbs on top. The fried bread crumbs were my newest invention.

And my mom tenderly kissed each of us good night.

# XII

From the window seat of an Eastern Airlines twin-engine prop, Jack Greenberg could see the Empire State Building and the Hudson River receding behind him. A tray with a salad was placed before him. He examined the salad very carefully, even lifting the lettuce wedge with his fork and looking beneath, before eating it. As in all his professional work, he was not alone. Beside him sat his closest friend at the Legal Defense Fund, Jim Nabrit, who worked with him on most of his important cases. Jim had been born into the civil rights tradition. His father was president of Howard University, the largest black university in the country, and had been one of the lawyers who argued the school segregation cases alongside Thurgood Marshall and Greenberg.[1]

A tall, thin man with a face pocked like a corncob sat several rows behind, and stared at them intently. He then picked up his newspaper, last week's *Montgomery Advertiser,* and started reading the funnies.

Nabrit reviewed legal papers, put them down, and began practicing card tricks. He turned to Jack and said, "I'm a little worried about this one, Jack. The mail room says we're getting more hate mail than ever before about this case. It may be hot in Montgomery."

Jack was silent for several moments. "Is your wife worried?" he asked.

"Very," said Jim.

"And yours?" asked Jim.

"Very. Very worried. More than usual. She has an uneasy feeling as though something bad's going to happen." He blinked.

Jim and Jack exchanged a long glance.

Jim suddenly leaned over Jack and pointed out the window. "What river do you think that is?" he asked.

Jack, without thinking, answered immediately, "Why, that's the Rappahannock." He chuckled to himself.

Nabrit looked at him quizzically.

Greenberg gave his tray with the empty salad plate to a flight attendant and pulled out a copy of *Rudyard Kipling's*

---

1. Jim had also become close friends with my siblings and me. He performed magic shows for us and occasionally took us to the races.

*Verse, Definitive Edition.* He tried to read, but his mind wandered. He remembered how as a young child he and his buddies had mocked the local Chinese immigrants and threw a rock through the window of a Chinese laundry and how guilty he felt afterward. He remembered accompanying his father, an accountant, as he visited clients and noticing that blacks never took the elevator with whites, only freight elevators. He remembered the "Jew quota" for entrance into Columbia College and being turned down for a summer job as a bank messenger because they "weren't hiring Jews." He thought of the tough guys who once cornered him on top of a large rock at the Bronx Botanical Gardens and how he had turned to face them, amazed to discover that he felt no fear, only intense determination to fight if necessary.

And then there was World War II. He remembered the names of each of the four black sailors on board his LST, a ship designed to slide right onto the beach to deposit tanks and marines. They worked as stewards, attending the white officers, making their beds, serving them meals, shining their shoes. Not "good enough" to serve with whites, they still risked their lives, manning their own gun battery. Jack had officered a gun battery—an antiaircraft, quad-mount forty-millimeter Bofors in a motorized gun tub—and when they fired at the incoming Japanese kamikazes, he could feel the concussions to the roots of his teeth.

Jack winced, remembering the invasion of Iwo Jima, the sky ribboned by bullets and explosions, and later, on the beach, the terrifying snap of sniper fire. Sinking to his deepest, most painful memories, he shuddered as he pictured the invasion of Okinawa, swarms of kamikaze planes attacking, his forty-millimeter Bofors firing without stop, making so much noise that he could not understand the captain's orders from the conning tower when the "cease fire" came. His gunners went temporarily deaf, and many cried when, for all their frantic efforts, the destroyer, USS *Drexler*, right next to them, took a direct hit and was blown to atoms.

As his eyes closed, Greenberg felt he was tied to all of this by a tugging string. The tugs were telegraphing him urgent, sometimes conflicting, messages, but altogether forming the course he had taken with his life.

The plane landed. Jim Nabrit shook Greenberg. "Wake up. We're here."

Nabrit and Greenberg walked through the Montgomery airport, and Corncob, who was directly behind them, walked into a phone booth and dialed. "They're here," Greenberg heard him say to someone on the other end of the line.

Jack Greenberg and Jim Nabrit took a taxi from the airport to the Banjo Jones, a dumpy hotel for blacks. Hotels in the South and much of the North were segregated and they chose to stay in people's homes or in black hotels when they traveled.

The Banjo Jones lobby was no more than a bunch of chairs with cracked plastic covers. It smelled of fried oysters from the neighboring po'boy joint. Gamblers who ran "numbers," an illegal form of gambling similar to a lottery, worked the pay phones by the stairs. The door to their room was hollow, and their beds sagged in the middle like hammocks. You could see outlines of the mattress springs not only through the mattresses, but through the threadbare, pilled bedspreads as well.

Yet the evening was a lullaby of jasmine and fireflies, the kind to make even old dogs wriggle on their backs. Wishing to enjoy the air as he prepared his notes for tomorrow's argument before Judge Johnson, Greenberg lifted his window and saw the Ku Klux Klan outside. Several Klansmen saw his window open and pointed up at him. One, sitting on the hood of a Nash Ambassador like a giant spooky hood ornament, circled in front of the building.[2] Its license plate, one of countless stamped by the state, had written upon it, HELL NO, I AIN'T FORGETTIN'!

Jack immediately ducked inside and closed the window and drapes. He and Jim pushed all the furniture against the door. There was a knock at the door.

"Who is it?"

"Mr. Greenberg, it's me, Banjo Jones."

"Banjo, call the police."

"I have called the police, and they ain't come. And what's more, Mr. Greenberg, the Klan says they want you two to come out."

---

2. This is based upon an actual incident in my father's book *Crusaders in the Courts,* page 141. He was in Orlando, Florida, to work on a case and "After dark, a procession of cars and trucks, horns tooting, confederate flags flying, some carrying blazing white torches, drove round and round the San Juan Hotel, where I was staying. A white-hooded, sheeted figure sat on the outsized hood of a Nash Ambassador, waving as it drove by. Before I went to sleep, I took the vain precaution of putting a night table against the door—at least I would be awakened if anyone tried to enter."

"Tell them to go to hell."

"If you two don't come out, Mr. Greenberg, I'm scared they'll be coming in."

"You tell them that I've fought at Iwo and this doesn't scare me." From outside the hotel there was an orange glow. A cross was burning and Greenberg and Nabrit could smell smoke right through the closed window.

"Banjo."

"Yeah."

"Call this number and tell the man who answers what's happening. I'll pay you back for the call."

Nervously, "Okay, sir."

Jack gave Banjo Jones a number in Washington, D.C., and prayed the call would get through. Jim practiced coin tricks lefty and then righty, leaning his back into the furniture barricading the door. Jack lent his back as well, and calmly opened up a collection of poems by Emily Dickinson, and, ignoring the noise and glow from the street, he read:

> *Somewhat to hope for,*
> *Be it ne'er so far,*
> *Is capital against*
> *Despair.*
>
> *Somewhat to suffer*
> *Be it ne'er so keen,*
> *If terminable, may*
> *Be borne.*

He closed his eyes and mulled the words *somewhat to hope for . . . somewhat to suffer.* Blacks had suffered so much. It would take more than hope alone to make their suffering terminable. It would take hope inspired by action. Action he was fiercely determined to take. He closed Dickinson and turned to *Rudyard Kipling's Verse,* opened arbitrarily to a page, and read the poem there, thought a moment, and reread it intently, bookmarking the page.

There were sirens in the distance, shouting, squealing tires, car doors slamming, then silence. Greenberg and Nabrit peeked from behind their shade and saw that the street was empty but for a large pile of smoldering ashes, blowing sandwich wrappers, and a police car parked in front of the building. Banjo had reached Thurgood Marshall, appeals-court judge, who called George Ribbon, a high official in the Department of Justice, who called the chief of the Montgomery, Alabama, Police Department, Nathaniel Hadley, and told him that he had better get his men down to the Banjo Jones Hotel *immediately* or it was his ass.

———⁂———

Roosters in a vacant lot puffed out their chests and proudly proclaimed, "It's morning, it's morning, it's morning." Dressed in his best gray suit, neatly packed in his suitcase by his wife, Jack Greenberg stepped outside his hotel, Jim Nabrit beside him. Two policemen who had been leaning back against their car stood up straight.

"Good morning, Mr. Greenberg," each of them said. "Good

morning, Mr. Nabrit. Chief Hadley has assigned us to escort you two while you're here in town to be sure you're safe."

"We're grateful," said Jim.

"Well, that's extremely kind," Jack said. "We appreciate it."

"My name is Emmanuel Jenkins," said one, a muscular man with a military bearing, a military haircut, and a civilian belly. "My partner's Luther Taylor."

Luther, so skinny that he almost disappeared sideways, had been eating scrambled eggs and oysters for breakfast and was speckled by crumbs of oyster breading. He had a startling habit of poking his bottom denture plate in and out with his tongue. "Welcome to Montgomery, gentlemen," he said. Both policemen had various epaulets, badges, and ribbons on their well-creased uniforms. Jack noticed that Jenkins wore a navy ring.

On the drive to the courthouse, Jenkins spoke up. "We know why you two are down here, and we don't like it. You're agitating the coloreds, and relations with them are difficult enough. But our job is to follow the chief's orders and so we're taking care of you."

"I notice you're a navy man," Greenberg answered.

"Yes, sir. Pacific."

"So was I," Greenberg said.

"What ship you on?" asked Jenkins.

"LST 715," Greenberg said.

"Never heard of it, though I saw a lot of the other LSTs," said Jenkins. "You see action or just do maintenance at Pearl, like me?"

"Action," Greenberg said. "Iwo, Okinawa."

"You were at Okinawa?" Emmanuel said. He silently drove. Then, sadly, "My brother lost his life there on the *Drexler.*"

"I was right next to it," Greenberg said, blinking. "We tore our guts out firing with everything we had, and must have knocked down two dozen kamikazes, but one slipped through. I'm terribly sorry for your loss."

Emmanuel looked back at Greenberg with reappraisal. "Thank you, sir—for trying to help my brother."

—∞∞—

The Montgomery Courthouse was a grand building with granite pillars on one side like a Greek temple. It had been built during the Depression as part of a program to create work for the unemployed. It sat above the post office and was filled with exquisitely carved stonework and paintings. The woodwork was indestructible cypress from the swamps surrounding the city, the swamps where escaping slaves had once hidden.

Before heading upstairs into court, Jack Greenberg called his wife. She asked how things were and he said just fine, no problems. Why, he and Jim even had their own police escort to keep them safe.

# XIII

*The Great Neck Record,
March 15, 1965*

## Police Boys' Club Tigers
## Battle Roslyn Warriors

Paul Ferber has a turtle named Polka Dot, who once got lost in his bedroom for a week until he found it in his slipper, but he is no turtle himself. Known for his speed, he is a fullback for the Tigers, a team sponsored by Great Neck's own Police Boys' Club Touch Football League.

Jimmy Hackenger, who can play guitar lefty or righty and intends to become a rock and roll star or, if that doesn't work out, an insurance adjuster like his dad (of Hackenger Insurance on Middle Neck Road), is a blazing fast halfback.

Jeff Anik blocks like a force of nature. He learned this

from growing up in a family with four older sisters who constantly attempted to keep him out of the bathroom, come into his bedroom, borrow his clothes, boss him, and even dress him up. He emphasizes that his sisters "tried" to dress him up, but never succeeded.

John Teevan, who blocks opposing players like the Grand Coulee Dam blocks water, was influenced by his family. He shares a bedroom with his brother and when tape down the center of the room did not work to keep his brother off his side, he built a barrier out of empty shoe boxes cemented together with pancake mix. When asked what brand of pancake mix, John admitted he didn't know, but his mom also used it to make waffles. When asked what kind of syrup his mother used, John said, "Aunt Jemima with Real Maple Flavor."

Dan Kozlarek is the team tight end, famous for his ability to tag the untaggable. Aside from playing touch football, his favorite activity is watching TV. His favorite shows are "Bewitched," "My Mother the Car," and "I Dream of Jeannie." In his opinion, color television is too expensive and "it will never catch on." After military service ("everyone in his family serves") he wants to become a 7th grade English Teacher at Great Neck South Junior High.

The mystery man of the team is Leo Jones, quarterback. He reveals nothing about himself, but the team looks to him as a leader with a deadly accurate throwing arm.

Last week the Great Neck Tigers took on their arch rivals The Roslyn Warriors in the last game of the season. Despite heroic play by all teammates, they lost by one point. March 27 there will be a team picnic at Cuttermill Park by the swing sets at 6 P.M.

—*David Greenberg*

# XIV

## Meeting of the Ku Klux Klan, Montgomery Chapter

Beside a neatly kept white brick suburban home, a Confederate flag flew over an enormous crew-cut lawn. There were massive, ancient oaks here and there, the kind that provided the wood for America's first warships, impenetrable to British cannonballs. An elegant river heron stood motionless on one leg, a living lawn ornament. It was early evening. The heron turned its head, and as if signaled, the crickets abruptly began chirring. On the slate patio in back, next to the swimming pool, frosted glasses of sweet tea clinked. A large group of well-dressed men and a few women were meeting: doctors, lawyers, bus drivers, store clerks, teachers, even policemen. They were all members of the Alabama Ku Klux Klan, Montgomery chapter.

There was a hubbub of conversation.

Duvy,
age eight, and
Jack Greenberg

Duvy, age twelve,
with his beloved
dog, Heidi

**ABOVE:** Jack Greenberg stands on the shores of Iwo Jima. **BELOW:** Jack aboard the LST 715 ship where he served as a gun battery officer during World War II.

Thurgood Marshall speaking at podium
as Jack Greenberg (right) looks on.

**ABOVE:** March leader and future congressman John Lewis attempts to ward off a state trooper's blow on Bloody Sunday. © *Bettmann/CORBIS* **BELOW:** A Ku Klux Klan member brings her son to a rally dressed in the traditional KKK robes and hat. © *Bettmann/CORBIS*

Sheriff Jim Clark proudly wearing
his "never" button. © *Bob Adelman from*
*Remembering Martin Luther King, Jr.*

Flanked by colleagues (from left) Fred
Gray (partially hidden), Bernard Lee, Peter
Hall, Jack Greenberg, and an unidentified
man, Martin Luther King Jr. celebrates
Judge Johnson's ruling to allow a Selma to
Montgomery march. © *Bob Adelman from*
Remembering Martin Luther King, Jr.

**ABOVE:** Participants, some carrying American flags, marching in the civil rights march from Selma to Montgomery, Alabama, in 1965. *Peter Pettus*

**BELOW:** State conservation department agents with nightsticks watch as civil rights marchers arrive at the Alabama State Capitol in Montgomery, Alabama, after a fifty-mile march from Selma to protest race discrimination in voter registration. © *Bettmann/CORBIS*

Martin Luther King Jr. leads marchers
into Montgomery, Alabama, on March 24,
1965. Beside Dr. King (from left) are Ralph
Abernathy, James Forman, Reverend Jesse
Douglas, and John Lewis. © *Steve Schapiro/
CORBIS*

"Give a nigger an inch and he'll take a mile."

"They're no better than animals."

"If we don't stop them, who will?"

"It's those Jews up in New York City who are getting them all agitated."

"Well, what are we going to do about this Jew, what's his name, Greenberg, and that colored lawyer, Nabrit? We showed them who we were last night and they just hid in their room."

"Cowards."

"It's this Vietnam thing that's got them all riled up. Why, that fellow Muhammad Ali says he don't want to fight and now the rest of them think they can do whatever they want. I hear that Greenberg and his boys helped Ali out."[1]

"That boy Ali can box, though."

"If we don't stop them Reds over there in Vietnam, we're going to be fighting them over here in our backyards. We have to fight 'em there."

A man with the kindly expression of a favorite uncle tapped a glass with a spoon, calling the group to order. His wife, a redhead with a generous sprinkling of freckles, bustled around him, collected glasses and silverware on a tray, refilled glasses, warmly smiled to all, and occasionally gave little hugs to those she knew well. The smells of lawn, lemon peel, and river water intermingled. The man spoke without introduction: *"The pur-*

---

1. For religious reasons, Muhammad Ali was a conscientious objector to the Vietnam War and refused to fight in a "white man's war." The government rejected his claim and threatened Ali with jail if he resisted the draft. The Legal Defense Fund successfully defended Ali.

*pose of our enemies is to diffuse our blood, confuse our minds, and degrade our character as a people.*[2] Now, y'all know that boy Martin wants to march from Selma to Montgomery here with a bunch more coloreds to stir up trouble. Says they should all be able to vote—as if they're smart enough to do so." Much laughter. "And y'all know that Jew lawyer Greenberg is down here to argue in court that King and his people should be allowed to march. And the question is, what can we do about it?"

"We could have a rally in front of the courthouse," someone said.

"Nah, Police Chief Hadley has gotten real touchy all of a sudden about our downtown rallies."

"We could send him a letter and tell him to get the hell out of town."

"Nah, we've sent him letters, and that hasn't stopped him."

Mr. Corncob, who'd been standing somewhat apart from the group, grimly spoke. "Folks, just leave it to me. I can't tell you what I'm going to do, but I have a solution for our problem. A final solution."

The man with the kindly expression looked at him thoughtfully and nodded knowingly, as did his wife. "Good, that settles it. And now my wife has a treat for y'all."

There was a phonograph scratch from inside, and all of a sudden "Dixie," the Southern Civil War anthem, started to play. There were giggles from behind the sliding patio door,

---

2. These words actually were spoken by Ross Barnett, a former governor of Mississippi, but are so apt I use them here.

and eight children ran out onto the patio and began what was clearly a rehearsed, synchronized dance to the music, like kindergartners on parents' night. Each of them wore a Ku Klux Klan outfit sized to fit them, though the eyeholes on some of the masks did not quite match up with the eyes beneath. There were oohs and aahs of approval from the adults. "And we got one more treat for y'all," the freckled lady said. Then two little girls, identical twins with straw-blond hair in pigtails, tap-danced to the music with precocious talent. They were in blackface.

When the music ended it was bedtime. Mothers gathered children to take home. Many tenderly kissed children good night.

# XV

Sighing, scuffing every step, I entered Beverly Bakery. I wondered when my dad would come home. I walked to the cookie sample corner. Through a window that opened into the next room I could see bakers in tall white hats busy over a counter dusty with flour. A giant mixer, like a metal kangaroo with a full pouch, whirred.

Mrs. Sutherd, eye shadow smudged on the side of her nose, examined a birthday cake on top of the display case.

"Can you do it in blue icing with white lettering?" she asked the lady behind the counter.

"Yes, no problem," the lady said. "And good afternoon to you, young man. Are you here for vun of our nibbles?"

"Hello, Mrs. Sutherd. Yes, please, if you have any."

"Ve always have nibbles for polite children," the lady said.

"And how is your father?" Mrs. Sutherd asked. "We've read about him in the newspaper and our congregation said a prayer for him."

"He's really great," I said. "He should be home in a day or two."

The lady behind the counter leaned down for her sample tray. I heard the door open-shut and watched the black student walk up beside me. The woman stood up smiling, tray in hand. She saw the boy.

"May I help you?"

"Can I get a cookie sample?" he said.

The lady behind the counter sternly said, "I'm sorry. There's no sample for you, young man."

"Oh," said the black student, crestfallen, and turned to leave.

"Stop right there," Mrs. Sutherd said to the black student, paralyzing him with fright. "Stop right there." Her face was red and the air above her corrugated with heat. She turned to the lady. "What do you mean you don't have any samples for him? I can see them right there. Give him one."

The lady behind the counter clearly was scared by Mrs. Sutherd's sudden ferocity, but also defiant. "I give cookies to whoever I vant. And I don't choose to give zis young man a cookie."

"That's racist," said Mrs. Sutherd, "and I will not tolerate it."

The black student's eyes widened and he turned to run.

"Stay right there," said Mrs. Sutherd, pointing at him with a quivering finger, freezing him in place. "I'm doing this for you and your people."

"What?" squeaked the black kid. "For Grammy and Grampa?"

"What do you mean, Grammy and Grampa?" asked Mrs. Sutherd, momentarily confused.

"They're my people in Santa Domingo," said the black kid, terrified, but also baffled.

"You vill leave zis bakery," the woman behind the counter said to Mrs. Sutherd.

"Make me."

"Go, or I vill call ze police."

"Good. Call the police. They'll arrest you for discrimination. You probably hate Jews, too."

"Vhat?!" screeched the lady, almost levitating in her rage. "I am Jewish. I am Jewish. A German Jew from ze camps." She seemed to puff up like a car tire overinflating, and she abruptly threw the entire cookie tray at Mrs. Sutherd.

"You're not Jewish! If you were Jewish, you'd have a mezu-zah[1] on the front door frame." Mrs. Sutherd hurled the cake at the lady, covering her face in icing.

"Zis isn't my shop!" the lady yelled, chest heaving. "It belongs to Mr. Beverly, who's Christian Scientist. Get out! Get

---

1. A mezuzah is a piece of parchment inscribed with a prayer and rolled up inside a case that is affixed to the door of Jewish homes to fulfill the biblical commandment to put the words "on the doorposts of your house."

out! Get out!" And she scooped a giant glob of cake and icing stuck to her blouse and threw it back at Mrs. Sutherd.

"Why didn't you give that boy a cookie?"

"*Oy gevalt, vey is mir, you meshugana meshuga,* because he didn't say 'please.' I cannot abide discourteous children. And I cannot abide discourteous customers. Get out! Get out! Get out!" she screamed, wiping cake and icing off herself.

The bakers ran out from the kitchen. They put their arms around the lady, comforting her. One handed her a towel.

Mrs. Sutherd bit her lip and looked back and forth. "Say something!" she said to me. "Your father's a civil rights lawyer."

"What?" I yelped, spraying cookie crumbs.

At that, the black kid looked at me and said, "I just wanted a cookie," and ran.

And I did, too.

# XVI

## King, Greenberg, and the FBI

As if on a tour at Disneyland, tourists walked a carefully charted route through the corridors of FBI headquarters in Washington, D.C. Through hallway windows they watched experts study crime evidence with test tubes and microscopes. Other windows revealed serious men, many smoking cigarettes, scrutinizing graphs and charts. From a basement waiting room, where a large poster read WE FIGHT COMMUNISM, one group of tourists at a time was disgorged to the shooting range. Behind bulletproof windows, FBI agents, nicknamed G-men, fired tommy guns at life-size paper targets of bad guys. Some lucky kid always got to take the perforated target home. There were concentric rings circling the heart, invariably shredded by bullet holes.

Seven floors above the tourist flow, two G-men, shoulder holsters bulging beneath their suits, stood at attention on either side of an imposing door. Behind the door was an office suite luxurious with dark woods and thick carpet. There were original portraits of past presidents on its walls and a Frederic Remington sculpture. The National Museum of Natural History was visible through the room's row of windows.

FBI Director J. Edgar Hoover always seemed angry and usually was. He was a short man, and seated behind his massive desk he looked like a bulldog on a booster seat.

"The threats against King continue," said his top assistant and intelligence specialist, William Sullivan, who was seated on the opposite side of the desk, a stack of colored folders before him. "They definitely are credible." He looked intently at his boss, trying to divine his intentions. "Should we let King know?"

Hoover gazed into the distance, tapping a pencil, the exact sort of pencil that tourists could buy in the gift shop below at the end of their tour, with the gold letters FBI embossed directly beneath the eraser. "We know that King and his followers"—and here he momentarily raised his voice and slapped the desk—"agitators!—are Communists.[1] Some are hippies.

---

1. The FBI believed that King was a Communist. This, not racism, was the basis of their intense hostility toward him. Sullivan wrote, after King's "I Have a Dream" speech, "We must mark [King] now, if we have not done so before, as the most dangerous Negro of the future in this Nation from the standpoint of communism, the negro and Communist influence . . ." Based upon this almost visceral bias, the FBI used illegal wiretaps to eavesdrop on King and sent him threatening anonymous

Hippies! They want to destabilize America. Wilson at the Moscow embassy tells me King was on the front page of *Pravda* last week. That Commie propaganda rag. They say"— Hoover's tone became mocking—"he battles American injustice. Now we're fighting the Commies in Vietnam. So telling King of this threat will only help the Communist enemy. No. No." Hoover smacked the desk again. "We will tell him nothing." He riffled some papers on his desk, calming down, read for a moment, looked up. "And what of this court case before"—glancing at his papers—"Federal Judge Frank Johnson in Montgomery?"

"Greenberg," and here William Sullivan opened and closed the top red folder. "That is, Jack Greenberg, director-counsel of the NAACP Legal Defense Fund, will argue the case."

"What do we know about Greenberg? Do we have anything on him?"

William Sullivan adjusted his glasses and continued reading from the red folder. "Internal Revenue Service files indicate Greenberg has always scrupulously paid his taxes." He muttered, "What else?" Then louder, "He graduated near the top of his class from Columbia Law School."

---

letters. The FBI used its influence to persuade universities to withhold honorary degrees from Dr. King and attempted to block the publication of articles supporting his cause. Instead, they looked for "friendly" news sources that would discredit King. Such was their antipathy that they even wiretapped, without warrant, his wife, Coretta, and continued doing so after his death.

Hoover said, "We must have something on him!"

"The only other file we have on him is his military record. He was a navy lieutenant junior grade on LST 715 that saw action at Iwo Jima and Okinawa."

"Go on," said Hoover, tapping his pencil.

William Sullivan opened a green folder. "His captain, Irving Trapp, wrote: 'Greenberg is an outstanding officer. He is extraordinarily focused and effective in battle situations, commanding the respect of other officers and the enlisted sailors. He is technically highly proficient.'"

"He's Jewish I assume, yes?"

"Yes."

"Married?"

"Yes."

"And what do we know about his wife?"

William Sullivan switched to the yellow folder at the bottom of the pile and scanned briefly. "The only information we have states that her maiden name is Sema Ann Tanzer, graduated first in her class from the honors English program at Barnard. There are tenuous links to Zionists who were running guns to use against the British in Palestine in the fifties, but they're unconfirmed. Supposedly her apartment was used as a transshipment point for light weapons. She teaches high school English in a suburb of New York City at Great Neck South Senior High School."

"Hmm. A Jewess. It's very likely that they're both Communists as well. Many of the founders of Communism were

Jews, you know: Marx, Trotsky. Lenin was part Jewish. Rotten Rosenberg spies who gave our nuclear secrets to the Reds were Jewish. So was Einstein[2], and we've got our eyes on Oppenheimer. Many Communists are Jews, so clearly many Jews are Communists."

"Sir, we have an agent, code name Dotty, working undercover in the Montgomery chapter of the Ku Klux Klan. She can't be sure, but she thinks there is a high likelihood there will be an assassination attempt on Greenberg very soon, probably by sniper. She thinks she knows who the shooter will be. Should we let Greenberg know, or should we take action?"

"No, Bill, the same principle applies to Greenberg as to King. They are aligned with our enemies and to help them would only give comfort to our foes."

William Sullivan tilted his head slightly sideways and looked at Hoover with a bland expression. "Yes, sir." He left.

Hoover stacked his files neatly. Then he picked up the phone to call Clyde Tolson, his assistant and domestic companion, to say he would be home late for dinner.

William Sullivan returned to his office, sat down, and steepled his fingers. A devout Christian and a powerful supporter of Israel, he considered himself an employee of a higher power than J. Edgar Hoover. What could he do? He couldn't say anything about King, who clearly was in league with Communists,

---

2. The FBI, suspicious of Communist affiliation, closely monitored and certainly wiretapped scientist Albert Einstein.

but Greenberg was another matter. Greenberg and his wife were Jewish, and that was almost the same as Israelite, a nation founded as a refuge for Jews. Sullivan picked up the secure phone, bypassing FBI operators, and called George Ribbon in the Justice Department.[3]

---

3. The above incident is fictional, but, in fact, William Sullivan became increasingly critical of his boss, J. Edgar Hoover, for what he considered his overzealous, illegal counterintelligence activities (e.g., illegal wiretaps, many of which Sullivan originally conceived and supported). Hoover fired him in 1971.

# XVII

The black kid's name was Donald Mirabal. The other black kid in the school was his twin. Born in the Dominican Republic, they had lived in the United States since they were little. Donald's father was interning at North Shore Hospital. We walked home together from school, sharing Donald's orange. He lived in the apartments not far from my house. As we passed the bakery he said, "I'm not going in there."

"Those ladies were crazy," I said. "Like the Three Stooges."

"Yeah, where Moe slams the pie in Larry's face. *Bam*."

"Yeah, right there in the bakery. *Kerpow*. Ha ha. Icing flying everywhere!"

We walked on, dropping orange peel in trash cans. "My mom went to college with Mrs. Sutherd," I said. "That's the lady who threw the cake. My dad says she's nuts, but my mom says she's just excitable. They shared an apartment when they were in college and Mrs. Sutherd was a gunrunner. She helped ship guns to Israel."

"Uh-huh," said Donald. "My dad is against guns. He sees lots of gunshot wounds at work."

"She acted crazy," I said, "but she meant well. She really wanted to help you."

"She didn't help me. My mom and dad went to the bakery to find out what happened, and when they heard I didn't say 'please' and 'thank you,' boy, did they get mad. At me."

We walked along, orange gone, silently taking turns kicking a stick.

"Blacks, whites. It's all they talk about," said Donald.

"Who?"

"Grown-ups."

"And Vietnam," I said.

"You watch *Star Trek*?"

"Yeah."

"*Star Trek* is how it's going to be."

"Huh?"

"I mean," said Donald, "that the future is outer space. We're going to colonize Venus. I read about it."

"*Popular Science*?" I said.

"January issue," he said.

"We need a moon base," I said. "And then we'll live on Mars inside giant glass bubbles. It's our only hope."

"Yep, only hope," he solemnly said. "But Venus is closer. First we colonize Venus. We may have to fight the Venusians, though. They're shaped like giant octopuses and they hate us."

"Octopuses. Uck. But we fight them there," I said, "or we fight them here. There is better."

"Yeah," he said. "What's with your hair?"

"What?"

"That greasy stuff in your hair."

"I'm a greaser," I said.

Donald almost choked laughing. "What? You're no greaser, and I wouldn't put stuff like that in my hair. You gotta let it be natural, like mine."

"I don't like the curls," I said.

"Man, you gotta have pride in who you are," he said. "I'm not puttin' no grease in my hair."

Donald gave the stick a mighty last kick, waved bye, and we parted ways.

# XVIII

The court bailiff rapped his gavel three times, asked everyone to stand, and said, "God save the United States and this
honorable court." The courtroom was dark walnut and smelled
like library books, an aroma Jack Greenberg had loved since
childhood. Greenberg was accompanied by his colleague and
friend Jim Nabrit and by a local black lawyer, Fred Gray. In
Montgomery, as in other towns, Greenberg worked with courageous black lawyers. They lived there and so had to remain
there when Greenberg returned to the safety of the North.
Fred Gray was ready when Greenberg needed help in Montgomery. He was the Montgomery lawyer who, in the face of
many threats, had successfully represented Rosa Parks.

Judge Frank M. Johnson Jr.—a former army infantryman,

still carrying a bullet in his body from the Normandy invasion—had a no-nonsense manner. He wore a business suit instead of customary robes and, instead of sitting at an elevated bench like most other judges, sat at the level of the lawyers, plaintiffs, and defendants.

The opposing lawyer, representing Governor George Wallace and the state of Alabama, spoke first. "Your Honor, the state is against King's march for two reasons. One, if King marches, this will agitate locals who may attack the marchers. If the marchers fight back, the violence will threaten public safety. And, two, Your Honor, King's march will interfere with traffic."

Greenberg conferred briefly with Nabrit and Gray, stood, and started his argument with the sacred words he had used countless times before, usually in Southern courtrooms, often in the Supreme Court itself: "May it please the court." Then in calm, measured tones he went on to say, "The first amendment of the Constitution protects Martin Luther King's and his followers' right to express their beliefs. The law guarantees them the right to gather in public and, with appropriate permission, to march to publicize their grievances. While it is true that they may be attacked, this will not happen if the court orders the police to provide King and his followers protection. Moreover, King and his followers have never behaved in a violent manner and will not start now. Their policy of nonviolence is well known."

Jack Greenberg then introduced King as his first witness. King stepped to the witness stand and took his oath to tell the truth on a Bible. Greenberg asked him what he meant by nonviolence.

*"One must have the inner determination to resist what conscience tells him is evil with all of the strength and courage and zeal that he can muster; at the same time he must not resort to violence or hatred in the process . . . never coming to the point of retaliating with violence."*

Hoping to preempt questions about why King's followers had marched on March 7 in defiance of the governor's order, Greenberg asked King to explain his group's action.

King responded, *"There are times that laws can be unjust and that a moral man has no alternative but to disobey that law, but he must be willing to do it openly, cheerfully, lovingly, civilly, and not uncivilly, and with a willingness to accept the penalty."*

The opposing lawyer, his voice dripping with sarcasm, addressed King. "Why, sir, should anyone believe you? You have been jailed countless times, which makes you an ex-convict. You have defied an order by the governor, sir. The governor! And Russian Communists often speak favorably of you, which must mean that you support Communism. And finally, sir, it is well known that you were to lead your followers on March seventh, but didn't even bother to show up. So, you are not a man of your word."

*"Objection,"* said Greenberg. *"The state attorney's manner is antagonistic and insulting."*

Johnson: *"Sustained. All witnesses in this court, regardless of who they are, are to be interrogated with common courtesy."*

*"I'm trying,"* said the state's attorney.

*"Make a little better effort,"*[1] said Johnson.

My father and the state's attorney spoke a bit more and the proceedings ended. They would have to wait the weekend to hear Judge Johnson's decision.

—⁂—

Officer Luther Taylor leaned against a pillar at the entrance to the Federal Courthouse, pushing his denture plate in and out. People walked past both ways. Cars buzzed by. The air was inexplicably tight.

"Stop it," said his partner, Emmanuel Jenkins. "Stop it. You're doing exactly what my aunt Miss Rose used to do. It's disgusting."

"A little angel told me something," said Luther.

"What're you talking about, a little angel? You're crazy. Watch for Greenberg. He should be out soon."

"A little angel told me that Greenberg's going to get his."

Emmanuel looked at his partner very seriously. "Is this some of your Klan bull again? I'm sick of your Klan, and that sponge-face brother of yours, running around in pajamas, taking the law into your own hands, scaring the bejeesus out of everybody. You're making things worse for whites and the decent coloreds, not better."

Luther snapped his plate in place. "Greenberg is a Jew, a Negro lover, a Northerner, an agitator, a Communist, a better-

---

1. This dialogue is taken from the transcript of the trial, which was recorded in my father's book *Crusaders in the Courts.*

than-you college boy. He's got no place down here interfering with our ways."

"Do you know something that I should know?" Emmanuel asked Luther.

"Don't know nothin'. But you watch yourself that you don't get in the way of things and get hurt."

"Darn it, Luther. I may not like Greenberg, but that doesn't mean I will stand for anyone taking the law into their own hands. I will not. I'm your partner, not your friend."

Martin Luther King Jr., Jim Nabrit, and Fred Gray had left the courthouse earlier by a rear exit within a knot of King's bodyguards. Jack Greenberg stepped out of the front of the courthouse and walked down the steps, cracked briefcase in hand, its buckle undone. His head was perfectly focused in the crosshairs of a Redfield Accu-Track Scope atop a Winchester Model 70 bolt-action sniper rifle.

Jack drew close to Officers Taylor and Jenkins, stopped, and abruptly leaned over to rebuckle his briefcase strap. A cloud of dust plumed in front of him, then there was the sound of a shot. Jack, knowing the sound all too well, ran, collided with Officer Taylor, who was also running, and the two of them fell. Taylor was already up and running when Officer Jenkins jumped on top of Greenberg, driving him into the sidewalk, covering his body with his own. The sidewalk cratered right next to them, stinging them with its grit, and again there was the terrifying bang of a shot. Jack was bleeding from the head.

Jenkins sprang up, grabbed Jack by the collar, and flung him behind a mailbox. *Bang*, the mailbox was hit, the bullet absorbed by mail and packages inside. Guards were swarming from the building now; there were sirens in the distance. There was no more shooting, just silence now, and the hum of distant traffic.

Greenberg was bleeding profusely from the head. Jenkins cursed repeatedly.

"You owe me twenty-five cents for each curse," Jack said, his voice slightly slurred. He'd fallen headfirst on Officer Taylor's dentures (which he kept forever as a desk ornament). When Officer Jenkins jumped on top of him, Jack's head had been driven into the false teeth, causing a spectacular yet superficial wound just below his hairline.

Guards and policemen surrounded them now. Three police cars screeched right up onto the sidewalk beside them. "Thank you," Jack said. "Thank you for saving my life."

"I didn't do it for you," Jenkins replied.

"You did it because you're a good cop," Jack said.

"No, that's not why I did it," said Jenkins, shaking his head, gun loose in his hand, pointing down. He was still panting slightly and was scraped and bruised. "I did it for my brother on the *Drexler*."[2]

---

2. This incident is fictional, but based on fact. There were many death threats against my father. He found out about one plot only after suing the FBI in 1993 under the Freedom of Information Act. The report "warned of armed men who would 'use high powered rifles, carbines, and other weapons and have orders to kill KING and GREENBERG. Armed men are also to protect and assist each other to escape.'" The FBI knew about this plot, but, probably out of antipathy for both men, did not reveal it, placing them in great jeopardy.

# XIX

My mother had her naturally curly hair straightened regularly at the Great Neck Beauty Salon. She confided that her hairdresser, Perry, a wise man, had recommended that she condition her hair with a mixture of raw eggs and Guinness stout, a dark Irish beer. So I tried it myself, whipping the two liquids together into a thick froth that looked so disgusting I figured it had to do my hair good in just the same way foul-tasting medicines worked best. I applied the concoction to my hair and went to sleep. The next morning I awoke and immediately felt something was wrong. My head felt heavy, almost paralyzed. I explored my hair with my fingers. But I had no hair, just hard crinkly plastic. I sat up and my pillow came with me. I looked in the mirror and saw that the goop I had put in my hair had completely hardened like papier-mâché and had glued my head to my pillow. I looked like an apprentice makeup artist's failure on a monster-movie set. It had not occurred to me that after applying the egg-beer mixture I should rinse it out right away.

Pillow attached to my head, I crossed the hallway to the bathroom. Ezra looked at me, staggered back, and yelled, "Mom! Mom!" Josiah stuck his head out of his bedroom, saw me, and howled with laughter. My mother opened her bedroom door and laughed so hard she fell to her knees and held her stomach. Heidi ran in circles. "Well, I'm glad I bring all of you such merriment," I said.

I showered with the pillow attached to my head and eventually it came loose. The glue in my hair softened and finally rinsed out. I shampooed to remove every bit of residue, dried, and dressed. I looked in the mirror and my hair was as curly as ever. However, it looked richer, thicker, shinier than before. Clearly Perry was a wise man.

My father called, something he seldom did when he was out of town because of the expense. Money was tight. My mom took the call on the porch, spoke in whispers, and walked to me staring straight ahead, no emotion on her face. "He wants to speak to you," she said.

"Hi, Dad. When are you coming home?"

The line was staticky. "I should be home in just a few days. I wanted to tell you something so you'd hear it from me first. Somebody down here in Montgomery took a shot at me, but I'm perfectly okay and I'm perfectly safe."

"They took a shot at you? Why?"

"Well, I'm working to get Martin Luther King permission to march from Selma to Montgomery, and there are people here who are angry about this. But the point is, I'm absolutely fine and you should not worry. Just look after your mom."

"Okay, Dad. I understand." And I did understand. I understood that my father, who had always been alive and healthy, would always be alive and healthy. Since he'd never been hurt, he never would be hurt. Experience completely reassured me.

"Any good food down there?" I asked.

"Amazing fried oyster sandwiches called po'boys," he said.

"Yuck, oysters."

"No, they're good. I'll make you some when I get home. They're like crunchy, creamy nuggets of ocean. Now, this call is very expensive and I've got to go. Let me speak with your brothers."

Mom, my brothers, and I loaded into the station wagon and drove to Grandma and Grandpa's in the Bronx. Heidi, who usually lay down in back, climbed into my lap and started gnawing my hair. I pushed her back where she belonged and she continued to lick my hair from behind.

Grandma and Grandpa lived in the same apartment where they had raised my father and his brother. It was on Decatur Avenue, a small asphalt street named, like many nearby streets, after naval heroes. Decatur ran parallel with the Grand Concourse, the major thoroughfare of the Bronx. Many of the buildings had fire escapes where kids or even entire families lounged. My dad told me that when he was young, some of the nearby streets were still dirt, and horse-drawn wagons delivered ice for iceboxes. He would climb over the tailgate of the ice delivery wagon for a shard of ice as a sucker on a hot day. Back then the neighbors were mostly first-generation Eastern Europeans, Italians, and Irish, but now Hispanic stores lined the streets. Wisps of Spanish music wafted from the Grand Concourse up to my grandparents' apartment-building door.

We walked over the lobby's floor mosaic, a blue circle with the number 10 in its center, to the elevator. The elevator, which always smelled of winter coats, slowly creaked upward. We knocked.

Grandma opened the door. "You're here, you're here, you're here. Come in, come in, come in. You've grown. You're so handsome. You look just like your father. Oy, I'm so happy to see all of you. I weigh all your letters. Your cousins' are heavier because they write more."

"But we fit more words per page, Grandma," Josiah said. "So we're actually ahead."

And then came the part that always scared my brothers and me: the kiss. We loved our grandma, but she had a wart on her upper lip with a short bristle that came out of it, and when she kissed you it not only poked into you, but it delivered a kind of bioelectric shock like an eel. We always tried to squirm out of the kiss, but Grandma would never let us cheat her out of what was her due. So we took our kisses with fortitude and my brothers sat down in the living room with Grandpa to watch *Gilligan's Island*.

My grandfather—former accountant, opera lover, avid reader, among the top chess players of the Bronx—had

Parkinson's disease and could barely speak or move. But my mother could understand him and sat next to him on the couch. Grandma was bony and taller than my father and had different-colored hair every time we visited. Today it was red, but not the red of normal human hair. It was an unnatural shade better suited to a Radio Flyer wagon.

Grandma led me into her small kitchen, taken up mainly by a faded yellow wood table and a large gas stove. "We're going to cook," Grandma said. "We're going to make blintzes, strudel, goose, stuffed cabbage, and your favorite, pineapple upside-down cake."

"Isn't that too much food, Grandma?" I asked.

"Nonsense. You're growing and you need good nutrition, not that frozen food your mother serves you."

"How about pumpkin pie?" I asked, knowing what the answer would be and pleasurably anticipating it.

"Ecccch. Pumpkin pie. I will not eat such dreck. When I came to America all they served us in steerage was stewed pumpkin, and I swore if I survived I would never eat pumpkin again. Did you know I came here with six dollars in my pocket? Did you know that I was so poor that I slept on two chairs put together? Did you know that I could have been a fashion designer but I married your grandfather and gave up my career for him? A fashion designer! And I raised your father and your uncle and I made them a hot lunch every day and a good dinner every night. And I made them do their homework, which is why both of my sons are so successful today."

Egging her on for the reaction I knew I'd get, I said, "Dad says he wanted to be an artist. He says that when he was in second grade he won second place in the New York City art contest."

"Artist shmartist," Grandma said. "I threw out all his paints and brushes. No son of mine was going to become a starving artist in a garret. And now he's the most important civil rights leader in America. He should have wall-to-wall carpeting and your mother should wear a mink coat."

"I thought Martin Luther King was the most important civil rights leader in America, Grandma," I said, enjoying her loopy thought patterns.

"Eccccch. Martin Luther King. What does he know? Your father is the most important and don't you forget it. And your mother should have a mink coat."

My mother walked in as Grandma said this, slapped her hand on her forehead, and immediately walked out again, shaking her head.

While she spoke, Grandma covered her table with a striped bedsheet and lightly dusted it with flour. Then she took a large clump of dough that had been setting in a bowl by the window, put it on top of the flour, and rolled it out with a heavy marble rolling pin. She and I took turns rolling and eventually the clump of dough began to turn into a larger and larger sheet of dough. Occasionally she would sprinkle just a bit of flour on top of the dough or under it if it began to stick. "You're done," she said, "when you can read a newspaper through it." Soon we stopped rolling and very gently began stretching the dough outward. And indeed we soon reached the point where I could clearly see stripes through the dough.

"Then you take melted butter and lightly butter all the dough, being careful not to tear it," she said, dipping a shaving brush reserved for this purpose in a saucepan of melted butter and very lightly brushing the dough with it. We pleated the dough like window blinds so it formed a rough rectangle that was many layers thick, butter between each layer. Grandma then took a knife and trimmed it into a perfect rectangle the size of the *New York Times*. She sprinkled a handful of bread crumbs on top. "You can put apples and sugar or farmer cheese and sugar in the middle. But I know your favorite is cherries. You have to use pie cherries cooked in butter and sugar."

"How much?" I asked.

"Oh, just a few spoons of butter and a few handfuls of sugar. Not too much, not too little. It must be just right."

"Who taught you this?" I asked.

"My mother," she said.

And she took from the refrigerator a bowl of cherries she'd already prepared and rolled them up in the dough like a long, chubby cigar.

"And then you bake," she said.

"How long do you bake it and at what temperature?" I asked.

"I don't know. The oven should be hot and you should cook it until it's done."

I looked closely. She had the oven at 350 degrees and I checked my watch so I could measure the time until she took it out of the oven.

We made blintzes, thin pancakes filled with cottage cheese

sweetened with sugar. "Could you use honey instead of sugar?" I asked.

"Eccccch. Use sugar. Honey's no good."

"Why isn't honey any good?"

"Because my mother made it with sugar."

"Okay."

And we made pineapple upside-down cake. "Could we use apricots or peaches or cranberries instead?" I asked.

"Eccccch. That's not right. You do it with pineapple because that's how it's done."

"Okay."

And we made goose, pricking the skin with a fork so the fat would run off, using the fat to baste it so the meat came out juicy and the skin crisp. And stuffed cabbage. I didn't even bother asking if you could stuff the cabbage with anything other than ground beef. Grandma was a great cook and a great teacher, but she didn't believe in experimenting.

"Look," I heard Josiah say, "they're talking about Dad on television." Grandma and I rushed in to hear what they were saying. A reporter in Montgomery was talking about the shooting attempt against my father. Grandma, clearly not grasping the situation, said, "See, I told you he was famous." Well, she was right and I was proud. And I wasn't worried. He'd told me not to worry.

My mother and Josiah looked very somber, though. Josiah closed his eyes and lowered his head. My mother walked over to him and put her arms around him and whispered in his ear.

We all sat down at the aluminum folding table that Josiah

and Ezra had set up in the living room, other furniture pushed aside. Grandpa ate the "pope's nose," the tail of the goose, something that always disgusted my brothers and me. (Ezra, horrified, said, "The arse!") Grandpa croaked some words, but I couldn't understand them. Sometimes when I didn't understand he would give up. He tried again and I still didn't understand, which made me nervous. But my mother said, "Say it again, Grandpa," and he spoke once again very slowly. My mother turned to me and said, "He says he's very, very proud of you for helping Grandma with the meal." And then my grandpa rasped out one more thing that my mother repeated. "He says you're like your father."

I wasn't quite sure what Grandpa meant by this, but I knew it was a compliment and said thank you. And then my grandpa rasped out something I was able to interpret. He was speaking to Josiah. "Don't worry."

Toward the end of the meal I asked Grandma about her mother. I wondered what had happened to her. Grandpa, who could barely move, turned his eyes to look at Grandma. "She was shot by the Nazis," she said. "They came into our shtetl and shot every Jew into the river. I had sent her the money to follow me here, but she didn't want to come." Grandma said this with little emotion and my mother signaled me that that was enough.

We kissed Grandma and Grandpa good-bye, and with arms full of foil-wrapped food, we left. Grandma's parting words to me were, "Oy, you have such nice hair."

# XX

Chief of Police Nathaniel Hadley was propped up on pillows in bed next to his wife, Clara. Both wore matching monogrammed pajamas covered in crumbs of sad cake.[1] They smoked Tareytons and watched *Lawrence Welk* while companionably rubbing toes. The phone rang.

"What now?" said Clara, toe-pinching her husband.

Chief Hadley picked it up. A distant female voice said, "Is this Police Chief Nathaniel Hadley?"

"Yes."

"This is the United States Department of Justice. Please hold for Attorney George Ribbon." Clicks and buzzes.

---

1. A Southern specialty, made by slapping down the cake every time it starts to rise.

"Nathan, how are you this evening?" asked Ribbon.

"It's a surprise to hear from you again so soon, sir," said Chief Hadley.

"I hear there was an attempt on attorney Jack Greenberg's life this afternoon," said Ribbon.

"That is true, sir, but we're on top of it. He's safe and sound."

"And exactly how are you on top of it?"

"I've assigned two police officers to guard him, sir."

"Two. And you think that will be adequate? Doesn't seem adequate to me."

"Sir, excuse me, but we don't require your advice on how to do police work. And I will tell you frankly that I resent your telling me how to do my job."

"Well, here's what I think," said Ribbon. "I think you consider Greenberg an outsider and an agitator from up north, and if he's hurt or killed you couldn't care less. But I am ordering you to provide substantially greater security."

"You're ordering me?" said Chief Hadley. "Well, sir, I just don't believe I have to take your orders, and I won't. I won't be intimidated by you."

"Have you ever had your taxes audited, I mean really closely audited?" asked Ribbon.

"You can stick it where the sun don't shine," said Chief Hadley. "I've always paid my taxes and I ain't scared of no audit."

"No, I don't suppose you would be," said Ribbon. "Tell me, how's Clara? I remember meeting her at the police chiefs' convention in New Orleans last year. A lovely lady."

"She's fine," Chief Hadley responded suspiciously.

"And if I'm not mistaken, her father's family owns a chain of hardware stores across your state of Alabama, am I correct? Fix-It Hardware, I believe."

"Yes, that's true," said Chief Hadley, deflating into the pillows.

"Well, I don't doubt that your taxes are in perfect order, Chief Hadley, don't doubt it for a second. But I do wonder if those of your father-in-law and every relative on that side of the family are. What do you think? Because if you don't immediately increase security on Greenberg one thousand percent, I'm going to send down a team of auditors for your father-in-law's stores, for your father-in-law, and for every relative of yours in the Okefenokee Swamp. And they're going to audit them down to pennies and nickels back to their weekly allowances as children. And if anything, *anything,* is out of order, I will direct prosecutors to show no mercy. None. Do you understand me, Chief Hadley?"

"Yes, sir, I surely do. I'll get right on it."

"One more thing," said Ribbon.

"Yes, sir."

"I have reason to believe that the shooter may have been a man by the name of Eugene Taylor, owner of a Nash dealership on Eisenhower Boulevard. He is identifiable by a pockmarked face. Would you please run a ballistics check between spent bullets and any weapons of his you can find?"

"How would you know this?" asked Chief Hadley.

"Oh, I have my sources. Thank you, Chief. And please give my affectionate regards to Clara. Good night."

Chief Hadley called the precinct and said, "I want a maximum security team on Greenberg now, immediately, pronto. I want him sealed so tight he has to get his air through a snorkel. And I do not want Officer Luther Taylor on his security detail any longer."

Clara asked tensely, "What was that all about?"

"Stinkin' U.S. Attorney George Ribbon was threatening us with an audit if I don't do what he says. There's an out-of-town Yankee who's stirring up trouble with the coloreds, and he wants me to mollycoddle him."

"We've never cheated on our taxes."

"Can you say the same for your dad and brother man and their stores?"

Clara bit her lip. "Oh. What are you going to do?"

"I'm going to do exactly what Mr. Fancy Pants Federal Attorney wants me to do."

Clara rubbed her big toe against her husband's. "I'm married to the smartest and handsomest policeman in Dixie."

—◦◦◦—

George Ribbon called Thurgood Marshall. "I think we'll see immediate results in Montgomery. If you hear otherwise, let me know and it will be a pleasure to set my hounds loose."[2]

---

2. This incident is my fictional creation. However, it has basis in truth. The FBI (and, on some occasions, the White House) did use audits as a means of intimidating people.

# XXI

Jack Greenberg put the finishing touches on his second-best suit with his travel iron, got dressed, popped two aspirins and a penicillin for his head wound, and walked downstairs to his waiting police car. Jim Nabrit, likewise dressed sharply, was by his side. Today there were three motorcycles in front of the police car and three in back, and the car sagged slightly on its suspension, as if overweight. It was. The entire back area of the police car—including the windows—was lined in phone books that theoretically could absorb a sniper bullet.[1] Officer

---

1. This is based on an actual incident in my father's career. In 1964, he was slated to give a speech in Mobile, Alabama. In his book *Crusaders in the Courts,* he describes, "About two hours before the speech, my Eastern Airlines flight landed and parked on the runway far from the terminal. A

Jenkins greeted Greenberg and Nabrit with warm handshakes and directed them to clamber over the front seat to the back "vault."

They drove swiftly to the courthouse, not stopping at the curb, but driving right up onto the sidewalk to the steps. Cordoned by police, Jack Greenberg and Jim Nabrit quickly stepped inside and walked to Judge Johnson's chambers. The opposing lawyer was already there and Johnson spoke without greeting.

"I have decided to grant Martin Luther King Jr. permission to march as long as certain requirements are met. Inasmuch as there is a question of impeding traffic flow, I would like Mr. Greenberg and Mr. Nabrit to outline in detail the complete logistics of this march. I want to know how many will be marching, where they will camp, what facilities will be provided for camping, including sanitary facilities, the exact provisions for food, water, garbage pickup, and security, which side of the road they will be walking on, their exact route within Montgomery itself, and the means of departure. I will expect this information by tomorrow morning. Good day, gentlemen."

The opposing lawyer hung his head and trudged out to deliver the news to the governor. Jack and Jim returned to the Hotel Banjo Jones, wondering how far a group could walk in a

---

car pulled up to the stairway, a flight attendant whispered that the car was for me, and I descended. Two black Mobile police officers, maybe the only two, picked me up in a car at the bottom of the steps . . . On the ledge behind the backseat the police had stacked telephone books, which they told me were there to stop any bullets that might come through the rear window."

day, how much water they'd consume, food they'd need, garbage they'd produce, tents they'd require. They began consulting King and his staff about how they planned to march.

King's aides wandered in and out of their room, providing them with information, stationery supplies, oyster po'boys, and coffee. Greenberg and Nabrit's document, crafted on a yellow pad of paper, was a macramé of fact, probable fact, and imagination. At one point Jack asked Hosea Williams how many portable toilets he thought they'd need. Hosea said he was unsure. Jack quipped that unless he could come up with a number they'd be singing "We Shall Overflow."

Greenberg and Nabrit worked through the afternoon and the night. They added one final detail very early the next morning: *"The marchers, upon reaching the capitol, will keep off the grass."* Greenberg went to sleep. Jim Nabrit walked the dark streets to Fred Gray's office and typed up the papers to be delivered to Judge Johnson and then he, too, went to sleep.

The hard work paid off. After reviewing Greenberg and Nabrit's detailed document, Judge Frank M. Johnson Jr. gave King permission to march. "[There has been an almost continuous pattern] *of harassment, intimidation, coercion, threatening conduct, and, sometimes, brutal mistreatment towards these plaintiffs . . . who were engaged in their demonstrations for the purpose of encouraging Negroes to attempt to register to vote and to protest discriminatory voter registration practices in Alabama. This harassment, intimidation, and brutal treatment has ranged from mass arrests without just cause to forced marches for several miles into the countryside, with the sheriff's deputies and members of his posse herding the Negro demonstrators at a rapid pace through the use of electrical shocking devices (designed for use on cattle) and night sticks to prod them along . . . The law is clear that the right to petition one's government for the redress of grievances may be exercised in large groups. Indeed, where, as here, minorities have been harassed, coerced and intimidated, group association may be the only realistic way of exercising such rights . . . the law in this country constitutionally guarantees that a citizen or group of citizens may assemble and petition their government, or their governmental authorities, for redress of their grievances even by mass demonstrations as long as the exercise of these rights is peaceful. These rights may also be exercised by marching, even along public highways, as long as it is done in an orderly and peaceful manner . . . it seems basic to our constitutional principles that the extent of the right to assemble, demonstrate and march peaceably along the highways and streets in an orderly manner should be commensurate with the enormity of the wrongs that are being protested and petitioned against. In this case, the wrongs are enormous. The extent of the right to demonstrate against these wrongs should be determined accordingly."*

Governor George Wallace made a motion, asking the judge to reverse his decision. Johnson denied the motion. Wallace then went to the court of appeals in New Orleans to ask them to overturn Johnson's decision. Greenberg, Nabrit, and Gray flew to New Orleans, argued against this appeal, and won. Wallace was out of options. He'd lost. King could march. Governor Wallace, a law school classmate and former friend of Johnson's, called him an *"integrating, scallawagging, carpet-bagging lawyer."*[2]

The Ku Klux Klan was so angered that they burned a cross on Judge Johnson's lawn and bombed Johnson's elderly mother's house. While, luckily, no one was hurt, the police had to guard both houses for years to come.

And Greenberg and Nabrit went home.

---

2. *Selma, 1965,* by Charles Fager, page 101.

# XXII

My mom put on her "date with Dad" perfume and we met him on the Long Island Rail Road platform. All of us walked home together through a spilled watercolor twilight. My mom held one of his hands, Ezra the other. Josiah was caboose. And I skipped around all of them, holding his briefcase in one hand, Heidi's leash in the other. After dinner we sat on the porch together and he told us about his trip, about the courage of Judge Frank Johnson, Jim Nabrit, Fred Gray, and Martin Luther King Jr. and his followers. Squeezing Mom's hand, he told us that she was the most courageous of all and she rested her head on his shoulder. Never once did he speak of his own courage. But I knew.

I lay in bed thinking about the evening and next Saturday's

Tigers' picnic. I was supposed to bring dessert. My plan had been to make it myself, but since Leo Jones had called me a jerk, I worried about this. Even though my father had told me that all the great French chefs were men, that Ernest Hemingway himself had invented a peanut-butter-and-onion sandwich, I was well aware that boys didn't cook, and if Leo Jones found out that I made dessert, he would mock me. Or, maybe everyone would think I was lying about having made it and they'd mock me. Or maybe no one would like it, or even try it.

My dad came in to kiss me good night and handed me his copy of *Rudyard Kipling's Verse*. "There's a poem here that I want you to read. It's called 'If,'" he said. "I read it down in Montgomery, really loved it, thought of you, and I've bookmarked the page. It's a very important poem." I promised to read it, put it on the radiator cover by my bed, and fell asleep.

# XXIII

## The March from Selma to Montgomery

Before their rooster crowed, before a finch twittered, before their alarm clock rang, Hector and Dorothy wordlessly arose as if tapped by different fingers of the same large hand. The windows were frosted, the floor was cold, and the hot water cringed within its tank. "Pipes too chilly!" Hector and Dorothy did their morning ablutions. Dorothy gently wrapped a long Ace bandage diagonally around Hector's shoulder and chest. And they carefully dressed in clothes ironed and laid out the night before. They wore thick matching sweaters Dorothy had embroidered with bells of Ireland—good-luck flowers—and solid walking shoes whose soles Hector had scored with a knife to give them grip. The alarm jangled, Dorothy swatted it, and they lightly treaded downstairs. Hector started putting final items—snacks, canning jars full of water, Band-Aids, and extra clothes—in a rucksack. Dorothy cooked a country breakfast of ham, bacon and eggs, grits, coffee, and orange juice. She baked muffins and served them with fresh butter and her own homemade beach-plum jelly.

Dawn arose, and in turn so did Martin Luther King Jr., Hosea Williams, and John Lewis. They joined Hector and Dorothy at the breakfast table, where all of them ate heartily and wordlessly. King looked at the others and smiled and chuckled, and all of them smiled and chuckled. A rooster sang out, birds began their song, morning spread wide her arms.

Dorothy quickly did the dishes. All of them stepped outside on the chilly, clear morning of March 21, 1965, and into Hector and Dorothy's Studebaker for the short ride to the Edmund Pettus Bridge.

As they drove, other cars, bicycles, pedestrians, and even people riding mules, almost all of them black, joined them in a happy, jostling flow, tributaries braiding into one river that temporarily stopped at the Edmund Pettus Bridge. Dogs yapped alongside them as though at a parade.

Journalists from every major paper in the country and from most major overseas papers waited for them. Photographers and TV cameramen filmed everything. And the Alabama National Guard, under President Johnson's direct orders, was there to keep order and provide protection,[1] bayonets fixed to their rifles.

---

1. George Wallace refused to order the National Guard to provide protection for the march and so President Johnson "nationalized" the guard and personally ordered them to do so.

King and his associates strode to the front of the group. Hector and Dorothy stayed behind within the happy crowd. They hugged and held hands.

Dorothy looked tenderly into her husband's eyes. "This is it."

Martin Luther King Jr. pointed, and all 3,200 marchers strode forward. It was fifty-four miles to Montgomery and the crowd, breathing out steam feathers in the cold air, was cheerful, chatty, and affectionate. People slapped one another's backs, traded snacks and drinks of water, joked. Many waved American flags. National Guardsmen walked with the marchers and military helicopters guarded overhead.

And yet, not all were happy. In isolated clumps on the road's shoulder, whites waved Confederate flags. Some waved placards that read GO HOME SCUM, BYE, BYE, BLACKBIRD, MARTIN LUTHER COON, MARTIN LUTHER COMMUNIST, YANKEE TRASH GO HOME. The marchers paid no attention.

Horses, mules, cows, and goats by the side of the road looked on in astonishment. Children ran from farmhouses and jumped fences to join the marchers for a mile or two. And the press, some walking, others in cars or the backs of pickup trucks, followed along.

"This is Dean Widdershins, and I am interviewing Mrs. Nemonica Nukkles, housewife and mother of five from Selma, Alabama. Good morning, ma'am. Are you and your son walking all the way to Montgomery?"

"Yes, sir, we are," said Nemonica, brilliantly smiling. "Every step of the way. And when we're not walking, we'll be dancing."

"And what does this march mean to you?"

"It means that Negro people are equal to white people. It means that we can no longer be pushed around. We are American citizens and we deserve the full rights of American citizens and that includes the right to vote."

"And what does this march mean to you, young man?"

"It means just what my mama said."

"Good day, ma'am. Good day, young man."

"A very good day to you, sir."

John Lewis undid the bandage from his head and stuffed it into his coat pocket. He breathed deeply, savoring the smell of the road after last night's rain and, from sheer joy, swatted Hosea Williams with his glove. Williams laughed and swatted him back. Martin Luther King Jr. laughed and turned around, walking backward, to see the crowd behind him. On either side of the road there were farms, mainly cotton, with dirt side roads leading to farmhouses in the distance. Here and there, atop circular mounds, were large oaks bearded in Spanish moss, like islands above the waves. And the road behind him, like a black furrow, cut through this ocean of farmland, as far as he could see. His people walked forward upon it, bounces in their steps. And as he peered to the limit of his vision, to the very back of the group, he saw cars, many cars, pulling up. Lewis handed him a pair of binoculars and now he could clearly see that whites and blacks were getting out of cars and joining the marchers. A car with Pennsylvania plates swiftly drove toward them and stopped. King and the Alabama National Guardsmen flanking him tensed. A white man and a white woman and a black man and a black woman got out. The driver honked his horn several times, reversed the car, and drove back in the direction of Montgomery. The four passengers simply joined the march, waving to King like friends.

Cameras clicked and whirred. Journalists took notes. "This is Dean Widdershins, covering the Selma to Montgomery Voting Rights March, which is much like a biblical trek through the wilderness. I'm speaking with the Reverend Martin Luther King and his associates John Lewis and Hosea Williams. Gentlemen, do you believe that this march will make a difference in the civil rights movement, or is it possible that the forces against you are too formidable for you to overcome?"

Hosea Williams: "The forces against us are the forces of hatred and ignorance. And the forces of righteousness and enlightenment will always prevail over them."

John Lewis: "We are marching forward to achieve the promise of America and we do not believe that America will fail us."

Martin Luther King Jr., watching from the shoulder of the road as marchers streamed by, said, "The road we are on is history. It leads from Selma, a town mired in the small values of racial fear and hatred and discrimination, to Montgomery, where a large future awaits us. We gladly embrace the responsibilities that come with American citizenship—patriotism, taxes, service in the armed forces—and ask only to share in the rights and privileges of our fellow citizens, including the right to vote, guaranteed to all citizens, without regard to race or color, in our Constitution. President Johnson has proposed the 1965 Voting Rights Act. This march is a megaphone through which we announce loudly and clearly and without equivocation that the Voting Rights Act is American, it is what is right, it is the future, and it must be passed by Congress. And Americans must march, as we march, to their congressman and senators to state this loudly, clearly, and without delay."

They passed all-white Southside High School, and though many students impassively watched them march by, others waved and cheered. Late that afternoon, the group came to the first campsite of the trip (a farmer's field), described in the march plan by Jack Greenberg and Jim Nabrit, outfitted with large tents, portable toilets, water trucks, mobile kitchens. The air smelled of moist earth, urine, and sweat. Hector and Dorothy helped set up a barbecue grill. A white Alabama National Guardsman, rifle in hand, approached.

"Y'all from Selma?"

"Yes, sir," said Hector, eyeing him skeptically.

"Well," said the Guardsman, "that's my hometown. I would like to tell you, ma'am and sir, that I am mighty impressed by you folks. I know some of my kin disagree, but you folks are respectable and I believe you are right and I wish you well. We need to put all the fussing behind us."

"Why, thank you, sir," said Dorothy. "We are cooking ribs; may I offer you some when they are ready?"

"Why, yes you may, yes you may." He walked away. As he did so a fellow Guardsman spoke to him.

"Delbert, we're here to guard the coons, not be their friends."

"Stuff it, Miller."

Some marchers played guitars and sang while meals were finished and cleared. Soon the encampment was quiet under a turning disk of stars. Hector and Dorothy, bundled in blankets on neighboring cots within an enormous army-surplus tent, the kind used for field hospitals, held hands for a moment. Hector blew his wife a kiss, handed her a daisy he'd picked in the field, and they slept.

All across America, people read newspaper accounts, watched the march on TV, and listened to the words of Lewis, Williams, and King. More and more of them, plain citizens and shiny celebrities, simply got in their cars or jumped on planes and came to join the march. The group grew and grew.

And on the day of March 25, 1965, twenty-five thousand Americans, black and white, rich and poor, walked into Montgomery, Alabama, flanked by National Guardsmen and journalists. Laughing, chattering, singing, they walked through outlying neighborhoods, past churches, past sidewalks lined with sullen, silent, white residents, and up the slope of Dexter Avenue to the white capitol building. Careful to stay off the grass, the marchers stood and listened to King speak. George Wallace, too, on his knees, peeking from behind his office window shade, listened.

# Our God Is Marching On

*My dear and abiding friends . . . and to all the
freedom-loving people who have assembled here this
afternoon, from all over the nation and from all over
the world.*

*Last Sunday, more than eight thousand of us
started on a mighty walk from Selma, Alabama. We
have walked on meandering highways and rested
our bodies on rocky byways. Some of our faces are
burned from the outpourings of the sweltering sun.
Some have literally slept in the mud. We have been
drenched by the rains.*

*Our bodies are tired, and our feet are somewhat
sore, but today as I stand before you and think back
over the great march, I can say . . . our feet are tired,
but our souls are rested.*

*They told us we wouldn't get here. And there were
those who said that we would get here only over their
dead bodies, but all the world today knows that we
are here and that we are standing before the forces of
power in the state of Alabama saying, "We ain't goin'
let nobody turn us around" . . .*

*Confrontation of good and evil compressed in the
tiny community of Selma generated the massive
power to turn the whole nation to a new course. A
president born in the South had the sensitivity to feel*

*the will of the country, and in an address that will
live in history as one of the most passionate pleas for
human rights ever made by a president of our nation,
he pledged the might of the federal government to
cast off the centuries-old blight. President Johnson
rightly praised the courage of the Negro for awaken-
ing the conscience of the nation.*

*On our part we must pay our profound respects to
the white Americans who cherish their democratic tra-
ditions over the ugly customs and privileges of genera-
tions and come forth boldly to join hands with us . . .*

*So I stand before you this afternoon with the
conviction that segregation is on its deathbed in
Alabama and the only thing uncertain about it is how
costly the segregationists and Wallace will make the
funeral.*

*Our whole campaign in Alabama has been
centered around the right to vote. In focusing the
attention of the nation and the world today on the
flagrant denial of the right to vote, we are exposing
the very origin, the root cause, of racial segregation
in the Southland . . .*

*We have come a long way since that travesty of
justice was perpetrated upon the American mind.
Today I want to tell the city of Selma, today I want
to say to the state of Alabama, today I want to say to
the people of America and the nations of the world:
We are not about to turn around. We are on the move*

now. Yes, we are on the move and no wave of racism can stop us . . .

Let us therefore continue our triumph and march to the realization of the American dream. Let us march on segregated housing . . . Let us march on segregated schools . . . Let us march on poverty . . .

My people, my people, listen! . . . Let us go away more than ever before committed to the struggle and committed to nonviolence. I must admit to you there are still some difficulties ahead. We are still in for a season of suffering in many of the black belt counties of Alabama . . . Mississippi . . . Louisiana.

I must admit to you there are still jail cells waiting for us, dark and difficult moments. We will go on with the faith that nonviolence and its power transformed dark yesterdays into bright tomorrows . . .

Our aim must never be to defeat or humiliate the white man, but to win his friendship and understanding. We must come to see that the end we seek is a society at peace with itself, a society that can live with its conscience. That will be a day not of the white man, not of the black man. That will be the day of man as man.

I know you are asking today, "How long will it take?" I come to say to you this afternoon, however difficult the moment, however frustrating the hour, it will not be long, because truth pressed to earth will rise again.

*How long? Not long, because no lie can live forever.*

*How long? Not long, because you will reap what you sow.*

*How long? Not long. Because the arm of the moral universe is long, but it bends towards justice . . .*

———ᘒᘒᘒ———

Within five months of the march, under intense pressure from the American public, Congress passed the Voting Rights Act of 1965, which outlawed discriminatory voting practices. Now the law provided a swift and effective remedy to prevent anyone from interfering with the right to vote. Local racist courts would no longer have power to obstruct a citizen's right to vote.

# XXIV

## Dorothy and Hector Register to Vote

Hector waved good-bye to Obadiah, his assistant. He stepped outside and closed the door of Milton's Engine Repair behind him. Both he and Dorothy, who had walked up the street to meet him, were church-dressed. They got into their Studebaker and drove to the Selma Voter Registration Office. There was a long line of well-dressed blacks outside the "Coloreds" door, and when they pulled up, people in the line waved, cheered, and motioned them to the front.

Dorothy looked down and saw that the flowers in the crack between the office wall and the sidewalk were now full grown, an explosion of color, many with their stems intertwined. One even grew indomitably from a crack in the plaster wall below the office window. Small ants were pulling away crumbs of plaster from the wall itself, slowly carving away the building's base. The shades on the doors were rolled up and the interior of the Voter Registration Office glowed, as though sunlit from within. Dorothy whispered to herself, "I'm back." Hector squeezed her hand.

The line moved forward and Dorothy could see the familiar woman seated behind the counter, madly smoking, lighting new cigarettes with the stubs of the last, handing out voter registration forms. Dorothy and Hector were three or four people away from the counter, when Dorothy looked over at the "Whites" side of the counter. The same clerk as before sat there, inactive. Dorothy grabbed Hector's hand and led him back outside again. Hector looked at her questioningly.

Dorothy walked halfway down the line, took the hand of the woman standing there. To her and all those lined up behind her Dorothy said, "Everyone follow me." She pulled the woman and the others behind her to the door that said WHITES. Without hesitation Dorothy opened the door and walked directly up to the woman who sat idle behind the "Whites" side of the counter. Dorothy said, "We are here to register to vote." The clerk was aghast. She anxiously looked over at her busy colleague, who didn't look back. She tapped her colleague insistently, but she still did not look back. The clerk stammered. She looked at the long line of blacks behind Dorothy. Finally she hesitated. She said, "Yes, ma'am," and handed Dorothy a voter registration form to complete.

Dorothy and Hector registered to vote. And in just a few hours' time several hundred black citizens of Selma, Alabama, registered to vote. And over the next months thousands and thousands more in Selma and across the state of Alabama registered to vote. And tens of thousands more across the South did the same.

In elections throughout the South, newly registered black voters helped elect black mayors, black congressmen (including John Lewis) and congresswomen, and a black governor. With more political power, black sheriffs, chiefs of police, and black school superintendents were elected and appointed. And all of them worked to put an end to much of the terrible injustice of the past. As a result of the increase in black voters, even the powerful Sheriff James Clark, who led the attacks against demonstrators on Bloody Sunday, lost his bid for reelection, ending his career.

# XXV

I watched King's march and his speech on TV, but mostly I thought about the Tigers' picnic tomorrow. The more I thought about what Leo Jones had said to me, the worse I felt. Words were extremely powerful all right, and one word had punched me in the nose and broken it: *jerk*. Why was I a jerk? Because I wasn't any good at football? So what? Because I said I would write an article about the team? Why should that bother him? I'd never harmed him, and yet he purposely insulted me. Was he better than me? Maybe he was. People paid attention to him. I was invisible. Perhaps it was my curly hair. The safest thing would be to buy cake and ice cream at Waldbaum's, make a brief appearance, and skulk away early. Yes, that was it.

It was almost midnight, and I was sleepy, but I picked up my father's book that I'd placed days before on the radiator, and opened to the bookmark, a card that said *Hotel Banjo Jones*. Oddly, the card and book smelled of campfire. I read the bookmarked poem, "If."

And I read it again. And again. The first verse of the poem seemed as though it was written just for me. I lay still staring at the ceiling, wide-awake, tingling from the words.

At 1:30 A.M., the house was completely dark and silent, though now and then the radiator clanked or gurgled. I got up, went downstairs to the kitchen, turned on the fluorescent lights, which startled me with their loud, momentary buzz. I took out *The Joy of Cooking* and read the standard strudel recipe. I mixed flour, water, egg, butter, and a little salt in a giant stainless-steel bowl, forming the mixture into a dough pillow, covering it with a moist cloth. Heidi came down, groaned, and lay beside me. What should I put inside the strudel, though? I scrounged the cabinets and found cherry pie mix. Not good enough. Canned pineapple? Not good enough. There were three dozen pears on the windowsill from the tree in our front yard. Mom was planning to dry them for snacks. I peeled them, cored them, cut them into slices, melted butter in a large frying pan, and gently fried them with butter and a little lemon juice, sugar, and then, stroke of genius, a dash of almond extract. I sprinkled raisins into the mixture.

3 A.M. I covered the kitchen table with a tablecloth. My dad came downstairs in his seersucker robe. He gazed at me silently. And then, not a word spoken, the two of us took turns,

and rolled out and stretched the dough just as Grandma had taught us. When we could see through it, we buttered it, pleated it, cut it into a rectangle the size of the *New York Times,* sprinkled it with bread crumbs, wrapped the sweet caramelized pears inside, and baked it at 350 degrees. We made several strudels. And as the strudels baked I asked him, "Why don't you buy Mom a mink coat?"

"Grandma," he said, smiling.

"That's right. Why not?"

"Why would Mom even want a mink coat?"

"Well, Grandma thinks she should have one."

"First of all, we can't afford a mink coat. Nor, by the way, can we afford wall-to-wall carpeting. But that's not really the point. The point is that Grandma is a wonderful grandmother to you and your brothers, a wonderful mother to me, but she has her quirks, as do we all. Grandma grew up extremely poor and so, from her point of view, wealth—and a mink coat is a symbol of wealth—is extraordinarily important."

"Isn't it?" I asked.

"Money is very useful," my father said, "but so is a meaningful life. Money without meaning is not the life I seek. I might make a lot more money as a corporate lawyer. But doing work I don't care about in exchange for a mink coat and fancy carpet isn't a good deal as far as I'm concerned."

———⟨∽∾∽⟩———

At 7 A.M., my mother padded downstairs and looked at us in amazement. There was extra strudel and we had it for breakfast warm from the oven. My parents drank coffee and I drank hot cocoa with a dash of vanilla. I couldn't help myself. It was an experiment. And then Josiah and Ezra came down and started gobbling so much strudel I had to stop them so there would be enough for the picnic.

I went back to bed and slept until late afternoon. When I got up I showered and looked in the mirror at my hair. My hair was curly. There was no denying it was curly. I towel-dried it, combed it, and then just kind of shook it out the way Heidi dried herself. Leaving the bathroom, I dropped the Score hair gel in the wastebasket.

At five forty-five, we left for Cuttermill Park. I put my strudel at the end of the big picnic table that was barnacled by large glass Coca-Cola bottles, potato-chip bags, bowls of supermarket potato salad and coleslaw, platters of celery sticks with peanut butter, plates of deviled eggs, and a giant bowl of fried chicken from Fried Chicken King. Paul Ferber stood beside me, tonging chicken onto plates, and next to him Dan Kozlarek served potato salad and coleslaw. "What's that?" they asked.

"It's pear strudel," I said.

"Is it a dessert?"

"Yes."

"Where'd you buy it?"

"I made it myself. Try it."

Each of them tasted a slice. "Incredible," said Paul.

"Unbelievably delicious," said Dan. Soon every teammate and every teammate's brother, sister, and parent was standing

in front of me for servings and second servings and third servings of pear strudel.

"David, that was the best dessert I've ever had in my life,"
said Jimmy Hackenger.

"Can you give my mom the recipe?" asked John Teevan.
"Strudel is ultimate. Can you teach me how to make it? It's
like Pop-Tarts, but better, much better."

Leo Jones came up and, without making eye contact, put
his plate in front of me. I dished him a slice of strudel and he
walked away without comment. Ten minutes later he was back
with his empty plate out for another slice. I gave him the last
slice, and still no eye contact and silent, he walked off again.

We cleaned up, made our good-byes, and drove home.

Later that evening, as my family read on the porch, the
phone rang and my mother answered it. She spoke, chuckled,
looked at me, chuckled some more, and handed me the phone.
"It's for you." It was Leo Jones's mother. Leo had loved my
pear strudel and wanted her to make it. She was calling for the
recipe. Before saying good-bye, she said one more thing. "Leo
thought your article in the *Great Neck Record* was great. He's
pinned a copy to his bulletin board. Thank you so much for
writing it and speaking so well of him. It meant a lot to him."

I entered my bedroom and walked to my bed. I was about
to crawl in when I saw on my pillow a small bag. I shook it and
it rattled. I opened it. It was filled with pistachios. I stared at
them, remembering that my dad had said he would bring them
on a special day. I smiled, ate a handful, and went to sleep.

# XXVI

If *by Rudyard Kipling*

*If you can keep your head when all about you*
*Are losing theirs and blaming it on you,*
*If you can trust yourself when all men doubt you,*
*But make allowance for their doubting too;*
*If you can wait and not be tired by waiting,*
*Or, being lied about, don't deal in lies,*
*Or, being hated, don't give way to hating,*
*And yet don't look too good, nor talk too wise:*

*If you can dream—and not make dreams your master;*
*If you can think—and not make thoughts your aim;*
*If you can meet with Triumph and Disaster*
*And treat those two impostors just the same;*

If you can bear to hear the truth you've spoken
Twisted by knaves to make a trap for fools,
Or watch the things you gave your life to, broken,
And stoop and build 'em up with worn-out tools:

If you can make one heap of all your winnings
And risk it on one turn of pitch-and-toss,
And lose, and start again at your beginnings
And never breathe a word about your loss;
If you can force your heart and nerve and sinew
To serve your turn long after they are gone,
And so hold on when there is nothing in you
Except the Will which says to them: "Hold on!"

If you can talk with crowds and keep your virtue,
Or walk with Kings—nor lose the common touch,
If neither foes nor loving friends can hurt you,
If all men count with you, but none too much;
If you can fill the unforgiving minute
With sixty seconds' worth of distance run,
Yours is the Earth and everything that's in it,
And—which is more—you'll be a Man, my son!

—From Rewards and Fairies, *published in 1909*

# XXVII

Josiah's hair fell to the small of his back and he pulled it into a ponytail with a rubber band. He had a wispy mustache and, though he had perfect vision, wore frameless purple glasses. Today, as he often did, he sported a paisley Nehru jacket, cowboy boots, and a necklace of wooden beads. He was a hippie. He had graduated high school and had started Columbia College the month before. It was 1969. The Vietnam War still raged. Forty-five thousand American soldiers to date had died there, and probably at least a million Vietnamese.

"I made you a sandwich," I said.

"Thanks, bro. Is it the peanut butter, honey, banana?"

"Yes."

"Excellent."

We closed the kitchen door behind us, walked past our pear tree, and headed to the Long Island Rail Road station, where Josiah would catch a train into the city and from there go to Washington, D.C.

"Since you're not going to be drafted, why are you going?"

"My college deferment," he explained, "doesn't mean they won't draft me when I get out of college. But that's not why I'm going to the demonstration."

"Why, then?"

"Because I believe, and millions and millions of others believe, that the Vietnam War is wrong and immoral. It must be stopped."

We walked in silence to the train platform, the air sharp with autumn's vinegar. We stood waiting for the train. "But why do *you* have to go? Think of Kent State.[1] They shot the protesters there. It's dangerous. Or you might be arrested."

The train was pulling in. Josiah said, "Remember years ago at Grandma and Grandpa's, when we saw the newscast from Montgomery about someone trying to shoot Dad?"

"Yeah."

"Do you remember that Mom whispered something to me?"

"Yeah."

"You know what she said?"

"No. What?"

"Well, she told me not to worry and that he'd be all right,

_____

1. At Kent State University, National Guardsmen shot students peacefully demonstrating against the Vietnam War. Some were seriously injured and some killed.

but she also said one more thing I've always remembered: 'Your father has no choice.' And that's how I feel. If I am to live a just life, I have no choice but to protest what I believe in my heart is wrong."

The train doors opened, Josiah boarded, and I watched him leave.

He, like 250,000 others on that October day, marched peacefully in front of the White House protesting the war. One of the songs the protesters sang was "We Shall Overcome."

Peaceful protests in America increased in size and frequency. And in 1973, the year Josiah graduated from college, the United States government, acceding to this pressure, withdrew all forces from Vietnam, ending the war.

I grew up and became a writer and wrote this book. I had no choice.

# Postscript

The story I have told is fictional. I have left out parts, concocted others, and rearranged facts and events. It roughly conveys a segment of my path to maturity against the backdrop of a moment in history.

The history is, in its broad brushstrokes, accurate, although some of it has been condensed and simplified to make the story more accessible. History becomes infinitely more complex when viewed through a powerful lens. In order to tell a story that is vividly comprehensible, I have used a relatively low-magnification lens. Some might object and suggest I missed important details, and that may be so. But I leave those details to the many who have described the times through nonfiction. The goal of this fictional work is more illumination than factual exposition and analysis. With every attempt at accuracy, this book highlights the emotions and struggles of the times and events surrounding Martin Luther King's Selma–Montgomery Voting Rights March. It describes many of the infamous tactics used by Southern officials to prevent blacks from voting (including the impossible test questions) and King's responses. It depicts, with reasonable accuracy I hope, family members' personalities, and my father's relationship with Thurgood Marshall, his interactions with Martin Luther King, and all that he felt tied to by an urgently tugging string. We did receive *The Thunderbolt*, newspaper of the Ku Klux Klan, and it did often refer to my father as "Vicious Jew Jack Greenberg." Thurgood Marshall did visit our house. Many of the words spoken by historical figures such as King and Federal Judge Frank Johnson are exact quotes.

Other characters, however, and their words are created for the sake of crafting a cogent, compelling story. Dorothy and Hector Milton are my creations, as are all the characters (except for those in my family) in my hometown of Great Neck. The phone call between Montgomery chief of police Nathaniel Hadley and attorney George Ribbon is concocted. However, it is well known that J. Edgar Hoover illegally wiretapped and collected tax information on many individuals in order to pressure them. And so the kind of interaction described in this scene seems plausible.

I have often inserted real historical figures into my story, such as Hoover or President Lyndon Johnson or his wife, Lady Bird, but their interactions and words necessarily are my creation, based on what they might have done and said. For instance, Lady Bird Johnson did not say to her husband in a helicopter, "Do what's right," but it's well known that she was deeply sympathetic to the cause of civil rights.

My father's childhood history, wartime history, and professional history are accurate. The stories are based upon my talks with him and his autobiographical book *Crusaders in the Courts*. And though the Ku Klux Klan rally I describe outside his hotel did not happen in conjunction with the Selma–Montgomery march, it did indeed happen at another point in his career, elsewhere. No one ever fired a shot at my father in the course of his work, but there were assassination plots. My father discovered one plot to murder him and King by sniper only after suing the FBI under the Freedom of Information Act. They knew about it and could have told him, but, probably because of their antipathy for King and the civil rights movement, did not. At another point in my father's career he did indeed travel in a police car lined with phone books to stop a possible sniper bullet as my book describes. He did travel by train with Thurgood Marshall and Jim Nabrit (who, along with his wife, Jackie, are great family friends), through the South. In some Southern appeals courts, he had more cases than most lawyers in those cities had. There was scarcely a major town (and many minor ones) in the South where he didn't have a case. And he worked with many fearless Southern lawyers like Fred Gray, most of them black. He helped to argue *Brown v. Board of Education* (among forty other Supreme Court cases, almost all of which he won) and he did succeed Marshall as director-counsel of the NAACP Legal Defense Fund. He represented Martin Luther King Jr. in court and argued before Federal Judge Frank Johnson. He did order a salad in a train dining car and found a dead fly on top and Thurgood Marshall interceded. He did (and still does) cook with me.

# Final Word
## by Jack Greenberg

"O would some power the giftie gie us to see ourselves as others see us," wrote Robert Burns.

Others call him David, I'll call him Duvy, as we did at home. Duvy's tale of his sixties' childhood as the son of a civil rights lawyer set me thinking. Do I remember myself at that age? What do I recall about Duvy when he was in elementary school? What do I recall about my father when I was that age? Duvy's story begins describing me aboard a lurching train speeding over uneven tracks. I am in a sleeping compartment, shaving, nicking my chin. Maybe that scene grabbed him because I often think of my own father shaving and told my kids about it. Perched on the edge of the bathtub, I watched the elaborate ritual. Shaving then was not as simple as now. Certainly, no electric razors then. His straight razor folded in and out of an ivory holder. Every few days he honed it on a stone, and just before shaving stropped one side, then the other, against a leather strap, massaging it up and down the strap. Then he would brush lather on his face, puff or poke his cheek out with his tongue, twist his mouth or carefully stretch his skin with one hand to make whiskers stand up straight. With the razor in the other hand he sliced them away.

Duvy several times tells of long trips, north to south and south to north on trains with exotic names, like Orange Blossom and East Coast Champion. The trains passed landmarks with strange names like Chattahoochee and Rappahannock. Lunch or dinner was in the dining car, on gleaming white tablecloths, plates, knives and forks clattering. A great constitutional drama played out around those trips and those meals. Before 1950, Southern racists had excluded blacks from the dining cars or dining at certain tables until the Supreme Court put an end to the ban. The racists enjoyed status by having a place at the table from which African-Americans were barred. One satisfaction I had from working at the NAACP Legal Defense Fund was that I was part of a team led by Thurgood Marshall that helped put an end to that cruel ban. I loved and told about trips on those trains in sleeping cars, which nowadays are hard to find at times, and to places where people want to travel. Today, compared to flying, the few sleeping cars are too expensive and slow.

I recall a school segregation case (*Griffith v. Board of Ed-*

*ucation of Yancey County)* in Asheville, in the North Caro-
lina mountains, that was heard during school vacation time. I
took Duvy and Josiah with me. We went in a sleeping car and
stayed at the home of Reuben Dailey, one of a handful of black
lawyers in the state and only one of two in that area. Duvy
and Josiah don't recall the case, but remember the trip. They
still marvel that Reuben Dailey's dog ate chicken bones and
survived. They had been warned not to give our dog, Heidi,
chicken bones, which could splinter and injure her innards.

Some of my cases came up in dangerous surroundings. Not
the Asheville case. I wouldn't have taken the boys if it hadn't
been safe. But there was enough violence, well publicized, to
stoke anxiety in a child who thought his father was at risk.
Duvy later heard of the Groveland case that occurred before
he was in school, when racist mobs shot up and burned down
homes in the small Florida community where two of my clients lived. The night before trial I stayed in an Orlando hotel.
Looking down on the street, I saw a hooded figure ride the
broad hood of a Nash Ambassador in a Klan parade that circled the block. The next morning I learned that the sheriff had
that night shot our clients, killing one of them.

Duvy describes a fantasy of an attempt to assassinate me and
my rescue by high federal officials. He would hear about and
sometimes on television see demonstrators in tumultuous confrontations with mobs and police. I was lawyer for the protesters, as Martin Luther King Jr. led them in Birmingham to protest segregation. I was his lawyer there, too. Police Chief Bull

Connor directed fire hoses and snarling police dogs leaped at them. I observed the clash from a nearby street corner in order to prepare my case.

Duvy learned about the Freedom Riders, whom I represented. To protest rules that required blacks to sit in the back and whites to sit in the front of buses, the Freedom Riders did just the opposite. At the Montgomery, Alabama, bus terminal, segregationists attacked them and set their bus on fire as police looked on and then arrested the Freedom Riders.

He probably was aware of James Meredith, who stayed in our home for a short while, the first black student to enter the University of Mississippi under court order. I was one of his lawyers. President Kennedy called up troops to enforce the court order. Two people were killed in the ensuing gun battle.

He may have heard about the time I gave a speech to the black longshoremen's union in Mobile, Alabama. Burke Marshall, the assistant attorney general for civil rights, warned me not to go. The Department of Justice had learned that there would be an attempt on my life. I felt I had to go because I should not stay out of harm's way when I was sending Legal Defense Fund lawyers into it. That episode is the source of a scene he describes: I'm riding from the airport in a police car, telephone books stacked on the shelf under the back window to stop bullets.

I'm sure that he wasn't disturbed by some cases that, while pursuing racial justice, also were fun. LDF successfully represented Muhammad Ali against the state of New York, which stripped him of his heavyweight champion title because he had been convicted of refusing to report for induction into the armed forces. But the state had given boxing licenses to many prizefighters who had been convicted of serious crimes. There was good reason to believe that race played a part in the denial. Then LDF appealed Ali's draft conviction to the United States Supreme Court and won on the ground that he met the test for qualification as a conscientious objector. Apart from undoing an unjust conviction, we got the satisfaction of a visit to the office by the world's heavyweight champ and tickets to his next championship fight.

But it is not strange that parts of Duvy's story are scenes of violence, expressing the anxiety a kid would feel about the safety of a parent. In fact I never suffered harm and have no way of knowing for sure when danger was real or imminent. But I never feared for my safety: not a rational calculation, that's just my personality. In World War II, I was in the navy on an LST, an amphibious landing ship that took the first wave onto the beach at Iwo Jima, one of the bloodiest battles of the war. My emotional makeup is such that I felt no fear—rational, but not normal, I think. I thought I would be shot or I wouldn't, and fear would play no role in whether that occurred. So I felt no anxiety during some of the most violent confrontations of the civil rights movement. But a child could feel very differently about a parent. I have a vivid memory of one night when I was perhaps six. My parents had gone for a walk in the park and left me in the care of a babysitter. A thunderous storm broke out, lightning flashed. I knelt alongside my bed and prayed for my parents' safety.

My father's work was not as exciting as mine as a civil rights lawyer in the South during the days of the civil rights movement. But because it was *his* work, it seemed important to me. He never faced danger as I did. But I recall graphically when he suffered back pain and, much more seriously, Parkinson's disease, from which he eventually died. A parent's peril is unforgettable.

A child who had been born in 1954, Duvy's birth year, could not in the early sixties grasp that he had come into the world at a turning point in American history. The Supreme Court that year decided *Brown v. Board of Education,* a case in which I was one of the lawyers. It made racial segregation unconstitutional, starting a modern process that continues to bring equality to African-Americans. Their slavery had been accepted by the Constitution until the Civil War and the Thirteenth Amendment ended it. But until 1954, the Constitution tolerated racial segregation, the aftereffects of which are felt today.

This book, a history lesson for some, is a nostalgia trip for me. I think not only of the battles of the civil rights movement that Duvy recounts, but of father-son days of that period. Duvy recalls and quotes at length from some of the poems I read to him. I read them in my father's books. I read those same books to Duvy. He reads them to his son, Sam. Somehow I must have transmitted to Duvy my father's love of storytelling. He invented a menagerie with characters named Archie the Ape, Gordon the Gorilla, Vivian the Vicious Viper, and Louie the Lobster, each one trying to outsmart the other.

Archie was the hero, Gordon the villain. Duvy has published a series of books about slugs, bugs, skunks, snakes, crocodiles, and other creatures.

Central to this book are the protests that led to the Voting Rights Act of 1965. Martin Luther King marched across the Edmund Pettus Bridge in Selma, Alabama, after Sheriff Jim Clark and his deputies had tried to stop them, beating them, running over them on horseback, jailing them. I led the lawyers who won the case that gave Martin Luther King the right to complete that march. Duvy tells that story as a child might have imagined it. There is some fiction among the facts, as there would be in the mind of a schoolkid. But it is essentially true.

—⟨≈⟩—